MISSING PALM TREE

Stories from America's Clandestine Service

W. BLAINE WHEELER

outskirts
press

Missing Palm Tree
Stories from America's Clandestine Service
All Rights Reserved.
Copyright © 2022 W. Blaine Wheeler
v2.0

This is a work of fiction. Names, characters, businesses, places, events, locales, and incidents are either the products of the author's imagination or used in a fictitious manner. Any resemblance to actual persons, living or dead, or actual events is purely coincidental.

The opinions expressed in this manuscript are solely the opinions of the author and do not represent the opinions or thoughts of the publisher. The author has represented and warranted full ownership and/or legal right to publish all the materials in this book.

This book may not be reproduced, transmitted, or stored in whole or in part by any means, including graphic, electronic, or mechanical without the express written consent of the publisher except in the case of brief quotations embodied in critical articles and reviews.

Outskirts Press, Inc.
http://www.outskirtspress.com

ISBN: 978-1-9772-5029-2

Cover Photo © 2022 www.gettyimages.com. All rights reserved - used with permission.

Outskirts Press and the "OP" logo are trademarks belonging to Outskirts Press, Inc.

PRINTED IN THE UNITED STATES OF AMERICA

For Those Who Serve in Secret

This book is dedicated with the deepest gratitude to the following:

The Stars on the Wall at Langley

and to

Bobby, an Air Force veteran, who listened
Phil, a Marine Corp veteran, who understood
Reed, a Vietnam Army veteran, who knew.

Acknowledgements

*Grateful acknowledgement is made
to Ariel Chart magazine for
permission to reprint the short story,
The Prisoner, in this collection.*

*I want to thank my wife, Nadia, for her
constant encouragement during the years of
compiling and writing these short stories.*

*My sincere appreciation goes to my typists,
Patty Dixon and her son Troy,
for their dedication to this project.*

TABLE OF CONTENTS

Introduction I
Missing Palm Tree 1
The Danish Island 19
Late Arrival 27
Near The Lake 47
The Street Lamp 61
Tower By The Sea 81
Night of Wolves 97
The Watering Well 114
Emigration Office 132
The Prisoner 151

INTRODUCTION

I wrote these short stories as a tribute to a man who spent 13 years as a clandestine agent for the Central Intelligence Agency.

Many decades ago I read a five sentence article buried deep in the newspaper about a government employee who had been severely wounded in the course of his work. A name, which I assumed was a pseudonym, and the town and state where he was were the only identifications given. I wrote a short letter thanking him for his service to our country addressed to the town and state without an address. I did not hope for a reply.

I received an equally short letter from him about three weeks later.

This began a cautious — on his part — long-distance friendship in which we, in the beginning, mainly exchanged personal information. I slowly learned snippets of his childhood growing up in poverty and a few things of his later life which I managed to incorporate into some of the short stories with his permission. I learned that he had attended two Ivy League universities as an undergraduate and graduate student earning degrees in German, French, Russian, and Arabic with additional studies in international relations and political science. He also earned a Phi Beta Kappa key.

It was always done by mail; he never gave me his telephone number. He had asked me at the beginning of this correspondence that I destroy all letters I received from him. I did that.

He eventually asked me if I would be interested in writing — in any form I might choose — about some of his work. He insisted that no dates, no names of the ones whom he extracted, and no dialogue be used. He also insisted that any distance and names of geographic locations be accurate. I agreed with his requests. I filled more than a dozen notebooks with the to-the-point and very terse information concerning part of his 13 year career. This took more than three years. He approved each short story as I wrote them.

I destroyed all the notebooks as he requested after writing the short stories.

One of the six readers whom I had asked to critique the short stories said that the stories were "too authentic to be fiction." The details of clandestine work described in the short stories are authentic; what is fiction are the descriptions of surroundings. The various geographic locations — when mentioned — are also authentic. Another reader correctly observed that the short stories were "chillingly accurate" because the travel and places mentioned are correct with both large and small details far too precise to be other than accurate. One reader found that the "actual behind-the-scenes information" clearly portrayed the mental work required in clandestine activities. The details of preparation give a view of the work which is "almost tortuous to read." Another reader described the short stories as having "a clear and dispassionate stating of factual events combined with suspense."

The events described actually occurred as difficult as it probably is for most people to grasp. There is little recognition of what most people could consider familiar. In fact, as a reader wrote, there is "a moral shock" in the reading of the short stories simply because the events involve what most cannot fathom having happened.

Yet they did.

MISSING PALM TREE

Because his last extraction assignment had involved his working with two clandestine agents from two non-friendly countries and also because four belligerents had been terminated, his debriefing at Langley took much longer than usual. He revealed that one of the foreign agents had used a high-powered laser as a weapon. He provided a detailed description of it. This information would be given to the ones at Langley who developed new systems. He also gave a minute analysis of the two foreign agents. This information would be given to Langley's clandestine agents. Prior knowledge was an absolute for successful operations. While Langley's clandestine agents did follow established protocols while largely working on their own, failures had to be kept low; and in fact, were not tolerated outside of some unforeseen catastrophe.

After his long debriefing, he was informed that he would have three weeks off before his next assignment. It was quite unusual for him to be given this much time off; however, he welcomed it since his last assignment had not only lasted a long time but also because it had been physically and mentally exhausting. He had not trusted the two foreign agents with whom he had to work. To make matters much worse, they did not trust one another because they were from two different countries with different field protocols. He imagined that they also did not trust him. Though the assignment had ultimately been successful, it had been violent with far too much time and energy spent on terminating the four belligerents who, he thought, should have been spared. In order not to jeopardize the assignment, he could not have contradicted the other two agents who had absolutely no compunction whatsoever in doing what they did.

He rented a small nondescript car in D.C., and began the relaxing drive almost 1,500 miles west to his parents whom he had not seen in more than a year. Whenever he could with enough time, he always drove rather than fly to an airport near his parents' home. He enjoyed immensely the long drive because it allowed him both the time to decompress and thoroughly clear his mind from the clandestine work he did. He never wanted his parents to see him immediately after an assignment. He wanted them to see him refreshed and unburdened. They did not know or suspect the type of work he did — and he wanted to keep it that way.

His parents still lived in the three room house far out in the country in which he had grown up. Electricity had not come there until he was ten years old. Water was drawn from a hand-dug well. They had fresh vegetables from their garden; eggs and meat from their chickens; also meat from deer, wild hogs, and squirrels; and milk from their Jersey cow. It was a life full of truly simple pleasures coupled with hard work, and it was an experience he would not trade for anything. It had actually prompted him to excel in everything from academics to sports. He was the valedictorian of his high school graduating class and a Phi Beta Kappa at the large state university. He excelled in track and basketball.

Several years ago, he had built an enclosed garage on his parents' property where he kept stored his 1967 Tri-Carb XKE Roadster. It was factory equipped with an AM-FM short wave radio and chrome wire spokes. What impressed him the most, however, were the in-board mounted rear disc brakes. While he was gone, his father started it twice a week and let it idle until all fluids were very warm. When he could, he thoroughly enjoyed driving the XKE on a frosty morning with the top down and the heater up. The crispness of the early day coupled with the sounds of the 4.2 liter engine's exhaust helped greatly in removing from him memories of his work.

When he was approximately 50 miles from his parents' home, he stopped and called them saying he would be there in an hour. He knew that they would have prepared a wonderful dinner for him: his father always cooked a big venison pot roast and his mother would bake a raisin pie — both his favorites. The 50 miles went quickly as he was thinking of being with his parents once again.

As he drove on the four mile gravel road from the highway to the house, he remembered vividly riding his bicycle on the dusty road. When he turned off the road and drove up the long and rutted lane to the small house on the hill, he no longer was thinking of his work. He was home.

The time with parents went quickly as it always did. One afternoon when he had been there for ten days, their telephone rang. His mother answered it and told him it was someone from International Marketing Services. While they believed he was an executive with this firm based in Asburn, Virginia, it was actually one of the sham companies with unlisted numbers the Central Intelligence Agency used. He could never tell his parents the truth about the company; nor could he ever tell them anything about his work. It was just something he accepted as part of his clandestine work. It may not have been an honorable thing deceiving his parents who had done so much for him, but his silence protected them.

When he spoke with the person from International Marketing Services, he was told to fly back to Langley at once. There were no apologies about his having to leave his parents so quickly nor were there any extraneous comments. When he hung up, he explained to his father and mother that an emergency had occurred at the firm and that he had to leave. They did not look too surprised since that had happened so often over the years.

They somehow accepted not only his many and long absences but also his brief stays with them. Both their stoicism and acceptance never failed to make an impression on him. His parents drove him 80 miles to the east to the nearest airport. As they said their farewells at the terminal, they told him they had enjoyed the ten day visit and that he was always in their prayers.

As he flew back, he wondered what kind of international emergency he would now be faced with on his new assignment. His many years of experience coupled with his physical and mental abilities would once again be tested. By the time he landed at Dulles, his memories of his aborted visit with his parents had largely faded; his mind was now focused on what might be required of him. While there would never be encomiums from Langley concerning his work, he knew he was trusted with the highest level of clandestine operations. That was praise enough.

He was punctually picked up at Dulles and driven to Langley's headquarters. The driver, as usual, said nothing to him as he carefully drove below the speed limit from the airport to Langley. Having an accident or getting a speeding ticket were not options. As he was being driven, he began to refocus his mind on his work. He seldom wondered what his assignments might be; however, this one had an aura somehow of danger. He would, as always, both accept the assignment and any inherent problems with it. Trust ran deeply both ways: Langley trusted him and he trusted those who made the difficult decisions concerning extractions. Assignments could not be completed without this mutual trust. Each side prepared very well; it was the unforeseen events which the clandestine agent had to work around successfully in order to carry out an extraction assignment. It was at this point where Langley had to trust the agent to use his physical and mental abilities to continue with the extraction knowing that the agent — working on his own — would make the correct decisions.

Before going up to the seventh floor of the headquarter's building, he stopped, as he always did for a few silent moments, to look at the stars on the wall poignantly remembering those agents who were killed on their assignments. They had served and died in secret.

Since the Director was at the White House, the Director of Clandestine Operations gave the briefing on his next assignment. The Director began by emphasizing both the strategic importance and danger involved. He minced no words as he explained that a successful extraction carried a low probability of being executed as well as a high probability of loss of life in the field. Communications would be very difficult and often impossible he explained. The possibility of any friendly air cover would be almost nil because of the various factions in the area — none of whom trusted the other. All of them also used civilians as shields. All had different types of surface-to-air missile launchers and used them often and indiscriminately. This resulted in a large number of civilian deaths and casualties. Langley could not be be a part of that under all circumstances he was told.

He would be sent to a small war-torn country bordering the Mediterranean. He would make his way once he was in the country to a small village, populated mainly by rebels with little association with any of the factions, located in the far northwest of the country some ten kilometers from the sea. He was told it would be very difficult to get there. He would be working with two clandestine agents from the neighboring friendly country. They were specifically chosen because of their very high level of competence and also because of their knowledge of the terrain and of the political and religious factions. They each would be armed with an Uzi. He would have a .40 caliber Glock.

The targeted person had been captured and tortured by violent revolutionaries who had no hesitation with executing their captives if they suspected a rescue was in the making. The director said Langley believed their very good communications came from runners who never carried papers and reported only orally. He was to identify as many as those he could and neutralize them. His two companion agents would be of valuable assistance in any runner's identification. When the extraction was made, they were to make their way the ten kilometers to the seashore where an armored speed boat would pick them up. The agent noted that the Director said "when" not "if".

He flew to the capital of the friendly neighboring country. There he met with the Director of External Intelligence who provided a very thorough briefing on the difficulties of the extraction. The difficulties would begin as soon as he and his two accompanying agents got to the border. They were to cross without going through border security. The Director's group would provide transportation to within two kilometers of the border. After crossing into the other country, they would separately purchase bus tickets at the border town which would take them to a small town about 25 kilometers from their ultimate destination where they would be given by a deeply embedded agent an old Land Rover Defender to drive as closely as they could manage to where the targeted person was being held. The Director spoke plainly about the danger of this mission. He made certain that the three agents understood that they were not to talk to one another on the bus — and if possible not to sit together. If the bus were attacked in any manner, they would have to improvise based on conditions. Each agent was given a small black shoulder pack made of the same material as body vests in which were advanced first aid provisions, ammo, gloves, and small satellite receivers. Thorough but simple Langley's agent thought.

The Director concluded their briefing by saying how very important it was to his country for the targeted person to be extracted. He was the leading scientist in their nuclear research program. The Prime Minister had made it clearly known that, if their mission failed, his country would without more discussion unleash enough force to kill all the ones who had taken the scientist. He expected the three agents to do all that was necessary to extract the captive scientist.

After the three clandestine agents entered the country by crossing the porous border separately, they bought their bus tickets and made certain they did not sit together. The trip to the small town took almost four hours. The bus was stopped twice by two different armed militia groups who boarded the old bus asking for identification papers from each passenger. As they got closer to the town where they would get off the bus, the destruction caused by airstrikes became very apparent. They passed through a village where, it seemed, every building had been destroyed. Only stray and emaciated dogs were seen there.

When they finally arrived in the small town, they made their way to a shop where kitchen utensils were sold. There were no customers; so all three agents entered the small and cluttered shop. They were met by the shop owner who was the deeply embedded agent who had served loyally the neighboring friendly country at great personal risk for several years. No introductions were made, and also no discussion of the mission was attempted. After being in the shop for a minute or so, and making sure there was nobody walking toward his shop, he gave the key of the old Land Rover Defender to the older of the two agents accompanying Langley's agent.

They drove slowly out of the small town on deeply rutted streets finding their way to the road which led northwest toward where the scientist was held captive. They knew that the approximately 25 kilometers would not go quickly. The so-called road had many detours because of bomb craters in the road. They met several trucks going toward the small town they had left full of refugees fleeing the airstrikes. Where there once had been fields full of crops were now blackened by the barrages of rocket impacts. It was a landscape devoid of life. It appeared that the only humans left to be seen on the trip were groups of armed militia along both sides of the road. The only vehicles being stopped and searched were the ones going away from the agents' eventual destination.

As they got closer to the village where the targeted person was being held, they wondered how long they could continue without being stopped and ordered to get out of their Land Rover Defender. Being stopped and ordered to get out of their vehicle would likely mean being executed on the spot. They had decided that, if they were stopped, they would attempt to kill all of the militia who had stopped them. They had observed that the groups of militia numbered less than ten armed men. The three agents believed they could terminate that few in a surprise attack while still in the Defender. It would be loud but deadly.

They had driven within five kilometers of the targeted person's place of captivity when their vehicle was marked by three close mortar shells and large caliber fire. If all three agents had not been mentally expecting such a surprise attack, all would have died quickly. As soon as the first mortar shell exploded about five meters from the Defender, the agent driving their vehicle immediately swerved to the right and slammed on the brakes. While this caused the mortar forward observer to call in a different distance, it did not spare the agents from the machine gun fire coming from the upper right to their vehicle. The driver quickly reversed and then sped forward to the left toward a wall made of rocks. He crashed through it even as the large caliber fire increased and the mortar shells were landing closer. Just as they jumped out of the Defender to take cover behind the rock wall, a mortar shell hit their vehicle setting it on fire. The quick action by the agent driving the Defender saved their lives. All saw the large caliber fire coming from the right across the road. They were momentarily sheltered from the machine gun fire by the rock wall. Four more mortar shells exploded near the burning Defender. The mortar barrages then ceased. After 15 or so long minutes, the machine gun fire also stopped. The agents had not fired one shot; however, the militia — no doubt young and untrained men — had basically wasted a lot of ammunition firing at a very thick stone wall.

For the amount of fire the agents took in the Defender, they suffered no major wounds: the driver had a long gash in his lower right leg; the passenger had shallow wounds in both upper arms; Langley's agent had a bone-deep bruise to his right shoulder. As they waited behind the stone wall for the militia either to advance or leave, they first assessed their weapons and ammunition. They found all were as originally issued to them. Only then did they attend to their wounds — with one of the agents watching guard while the wounds of the other two were cared for. When the agent standing guard was being bandaged, another agent took his place. The greatest loss was the mobile GPS unit which was destroyed in the burning Defender. They now had no direct communication with anyone anywhere. Their movements, however, would be tracked by both Langley's and the other intelligence group's satellites through their receivers in their small shoulder packs.

After seeing and ascertaining for certain that the attacking militia had left their area and that there were no more in-coming mortar rounds, they left the cover of the stone wall and ran toward a partially destroyed and abandoned stone house. The house had no roof, door, or windows; in fact, all that was left of what had been a farmer's house were the thick stone walls. It had obviously been constructed by the farmer one heavy stone at a time. It measured perhaps six meters square. The floor was packed dirt. Near one of what would have been a window was a circular fire pit made of smaller stones. It, no doubt, served as the place where their food was cooked.

As they entered the house, they were met by an overpowering and relentless odor of decaying human flesh. It was pervasive even with no roof which allowed some of the stench to escape. The three agents quickly found the source: in a corner farthest from what was once the only door lay three corpses crumpled together in a grotesque pile with huge rats chewing on the bodies. One was a man who had attempted in vain to shield his wife and young child from the murderous hail of bullets when a militia group had burst in. The militia had then, to add a concluding insult to a grievous deed, set fire to the low and wooden roof and tore the door off its hinges. The three agents, all inured by years of categorical death and destruction, found the scene difficult both to understand and accept. The agents agreed together with a calm but seething fury that they would terminate as many of the militia they could on this assignment.

Since it was now dusk and with no sounds or signs of any approaching militia, they decided they would wait outside the house until it became fully dark. Before they left the house, they placed the large door over the bodies of the family. All regretted that they could not kill the rats. They hoped that relatives might find the bodies and give the family a proper burial.

They left the house around 9:00pm walking silently and quickly in the darkness about five meters from the road. There were some empty irrigation ditches and a few small fields of fava beans but nothing difficult to impede their determined walk to the house where the scientist was being held. They knew it would be closely guarded by heavily armed men. The moon was barely a crescent which provided the agents with an almost complete cover of darkness. Langley's agent had night vision goggles; so he took the point.

They covered the five kilometers to the small village quickly and located the house which fortunately was on the northwest outskirts of the village. This meant that, once the extraction had been accomplished, they would not have to circumvent the village but begin their walk with the targeted person the ten or so kilometers to the sea coast where all four would be picked up.

When they were about 20 meters from the house, Langley's agent signaled for the other two agents to stop. With his night vision goggles he had spied a trip wire attached to a palm tree. It went in both directions about 15 meters from the house. They decided to follow the wire leading to their left. It circled the house entirely being wrapped around palm trees about 20 meters apart. Each palm tree had an explosive tied to it. The wire ended at a missing palm tree where both ends of the trip wire were attached to a large cache of explosives. They decided they would split up in equidistance from each other around the house. They would each fire one round into the explosive tied to a palm tree. Langley's agent would fire into the large cache. They believed the resulting explosions would empty the house of the guards. Each agent would terminate as many armed men as he could. They knew for certain two things: the three explosions from three different directions would take the militia by total surprise, and the armed men would rush toward the three explosions. This would expose them to the agents' deadly fire. Langley's agent would enter the house and rescue the scientist. All would rendezvous near the area of the large cache.

They synchronized their watches and allotted 30 seconds for each to be in place. If any of the agents had to terminate anyone prior to getting to his place, it would be with a knife. Each understood that, in order to rescue the scientist, most — if not all — of the armed men in and around the house would have to be terminated quickly and efficiently. The satellite photos of both Langley and the other agents' intelligence groups indicated that there were 20 to 24 heavily armed militia in the proximate area. Those are good odds for us Langley's agent thought. Not only would they have the advantage of the explosions to disrupt the reactions of the militia but they would also have the element of surprise since none of the militia knew of the presence of the three agents. As the militia in the house would spill out of the house and any outside would not know accurately the direction of the agents' attack, it would be a matter of terminating them as quickly as possible. They also believed from experience that the targeted person would be left alone since any guarding him would also run outside. The agent would then terminate everyone he could in his sector and then sprint into the house to rescue the targeted person. He hoped there would be no booby traps attached to the scientist. It was a chance he not only would be taking but also one he could not refuse to do.

At exactly 30 seconds each agent fired his one round into the explosives near him. Each had lain flat on the well-trodden and dusty ground taking cover behind anything which might provide more protection. They knew that the militia would be firing indiscriminately in front of them as they ran out. By lying flat the agents could add another deadly element in their surprise attack. They would remain lying down as long as they could. They believed they could, with a heavy barrage of fire, terminate all of them.

As soon as the three explosions occurred, the house with the militia inside and those napping outside erupted with shouts indicating confusion. None knew where the attackers were or, for that matter, how many there were. In the confusion some of the militia outside were shot and killed by the ones running out of the house firing without looking or thinking. Since there were three explosions in different areas around the house, the untrained militia, instead of splitting up and concentrating their fire on the three areas, ran back and forth without any order. They were firing in all directions all the while wasting their ammunition. There appeared to be no one who took command of them. The agents' surprise attack had worked perfectly.

When the other two agents saw that militia had not come around the house to their positions, they moved in opposite directions resulting in a classic pincher movement. As they came around the house from opposite directions, they caught the militia in a deadly crossfire. They moved swiftly toward the area where Langley's agent was. By the time they got to his area, he was already in the house rescuing the scientist. They remained outside in the event more militia showed up.

The agent saw that none of the militia went to the sides of the house. He also knew that the other two agents would quickly recognize this mistake and take fast offensive action. When he saw the effects of their crossfire, he knew that he would be able to go into the house easily. By the time he had emptied and reloaded his Glock, the other agents had terminated the remainder. He got up from his prone position and sprinted the 15 meters to the door of the house through the acrid smoke of the fired weapons.

He found the scientist lying on a filthy mattress with only soiled underwear covering his emaciated and sore-infested body. He knew the man would be unable to walk; so he picked him up, noticing at once that he had a sweet smelling oder to his breath, and carried him out to the other agents who spoke to him in his language. They assured him that he was safe and that they would get him back home soon. One of the agents gently took him from the arms of Langley's agent and held the scientist almost as though he were a small child.

From the moment they fired their one shot each into the explosives to the successful rescue of the nuclear scientist, it took less than three minutes. They left behind 22 dead militia.

Since Langley's agent had his night vision goggles, he led the way from the house on their approximately ten kilometer double-time walk in the sea. They could not afford to stop on the way. Prior to leaving, the other agents carefully gave the scientist some water and part of a protein bar as they once again assured him that he would soon be safely home. He was too weak to answer. All three agents hoped the frail man would survive. Once on the armored speed boat, he would be attended to by a government physician. They would both protect and take care of him until then.

There was one small village according to the satellite photos between their location and the sea. While there were no indications of militia in the village or nearby, all three agents knew that goats, dogs, donkeys, and perhaps other animals would be in and near the village. They would have to make a large detour around it. They did not want to awaken any animal which, in turn, would awaken some inhabitants with their sounds. They also did not want to harm innocent villagers. On an almost moonless night both humans and animals would likely be asleep.

According to the satellite photos, the village was nestled on the north against a small hill which extended to the east but not to the north. Approximately 100 meters to the south of the village, there was a sloping ravine with one narrow path down to flat ground. The gradient was rather steep, but they had no choice but to take this route. The ravine extended too far to the south for them to use precious time getting around it. Each of the agents recognized the difficulty they would face going down a fairly steep and rocky path. There was no discussion of the alternative; they accepted the expedient with its difficulties.

As they carefully — and as quickly as they could — descended the narrow and steep path to the bottom of the ravine, the foreign agent carrying the scientist told the other two agents in a loud whisper that the man was having difficulty breathing and was also becoming delirious. They stopped their decent momentarily in order to give him some more water and also to pour some of their limited amount of water over the head of the scientist. It seemed to calm him even though he continued his labored breathing. His breath had the smell of a diabetic.

They knew that somehow they had to accelerate their already quick walk to pick-up spot without harming the man. They managed to get down the ravine's path without sliding on the small stones on it.

When they reached level ground, they stopped for perhaps 30 seconds. The foreign agent who had been carrying the scientist gave him to his compatriot to carry. He told the other two agents that he would be able to run carrying the weakened and failing man the approximately four kilometers to the sea. He assured the other two agents that he could sprint that distance carrying the scientist. They all then agreed to sprint following closely Langley's agent who led the way with his night vision goggles.

Though they were now approaching physical exhaustion, they found the will to urge their bodies to greater effort. They knew the life of the scientist depended on them.

When they were perhaps one kilometer from the sea where they would be picked up, Langley's agent halted their tiring sprint because there was a small herd of goats lying on the narrow trail. They slowly approached the herd taking care they did not disturb them so that none would butt or kick the agent carrying the scientist. The slow progress helped the agents recover their fast depleting strength; although, the slow progress did not help their rescued person. They managed to pick their way through the herd without stumbling or being butted. As soon as they got through the goats, they sprinted even faster toward the sea.

As they approached the sea, they found that the beach area was full of large and slippery rocks. They had to slow down for the last 50 meters so that they would not fall. When they got to the sea's edge, they saw one small blinking light about 15 meters from the shore. It was on a large rubber dinghy which had been launched from the armored speed boat. It was to their left where some sand was rather than slippery rocks were. They moved as quickly with caution as they could toward the dinghy. The coxswain steered it as closely as he could to the shore using all of the shallow water as possible. There were three other people in it. All were armed with Uzis. The three agents were thankful their small satellite receivers had pinpointed their location.

The foreign agent carrying the scientist went first into the warm and shallow water. He lifted the man up to one of the men on the dinghy who cradled him closely to his body. Very quickly a woolen blanket was placed over the scientist. He was also given sugared water. He was incoherent and shivering. The agents hoped he was not going into a diabetic shock. Langley's agent told the ones on the dinghy that, when he first picked the targeted person up, he had a sweet smelling breath. They told him the scientist was diabetic before he was abducted, and he would be treated on the large speed boat by a physician. All knew he had not been given insulin by the militia.

The dinghy raced to the armored speed boat which was lying broadside some 30 meters from the shore. The extracted scientist was quickly and as carefully as possible transferred to the speed boat. As soon as everyone had left the dinghy, which had been roped to the speed boat, a seaman threw three heavy blocks of cement into it; undid the fastening ropes; and then pulled a cord attached to the middle of the dinghy. This set off a muted underwater explosion which caused the dinghy to sink almost immediately. This action would leave no evidence of the sea rescue. Very well done Langley's agent thought.

While the armored speed boat raced at full throttle hugging the coast to the waters of the friendly neighboring nation, a physician attended to the scientist by administering insulin and other medications. His filthy and lice-infected underwear was removed. He was given an alcohol bath using small white towels which quickly became dark with both dirt and scabs from his body. After bathing him, another man gently put a soft cotton robe on him. By the time the speed boat had docked, his long and curved fingernails and toenails had been clipped. His scraggy beard had been shaved off and his hair trimmed. Langley's agent noticed that, before everything had been done to the scientist, many photos of him in his deplorable condition were taken. He knew those photos would be used as evidence of torture and maltreatment when the main group supporting the militia would attempt to tell the world that they did not torture any captives.

When the speed boat was safely docked, the extracted nuclear scientist was removed on a stretcher and taken to a waiting ambulance. The three agents then disembarked and walked to a government-plated black SUV and were swiftly driven to the plain building housing the Director of External Intelligence. There they showered and shaved and were given fresh clothing and shoes. All three agents also turned in their weapons and small shoulder packs. They were then ushered into the Director's office.

As soon as the three agents entered the Director's office, he got up from his spartan metal desk and shook their hands. He thanked each agent individually while they were standing. He then motioned for them to sit in chairs facing the thick door of his office. He told them what all three had heard before: that, while their work was exemplary and useful to the country, it could never be made public — nor could their names ever be mentioned. He told Langley's agent that he was certain he would hear the same thing. He also said he was grateful for the cooperation between the two countries' intelligence groups. He concluded by saying with a wry smile that he hoped each would now have some time off before their next assignments. He stood up; shook their hands again; and the three agents left his office without having said a word.

Since he had worked with foreign agents and had terminated belligerents on this extraction, he would not be able to give his debriefing at an American embassy. It was a required protocol that he return to Langley for his debriefing. As he left the friendly country, he wondered what his parents were doing. He also hoped that he could see them again before his next extraction assignment. Time, it seemed, was never on his side.

THE DANISH ISLAND

The agent had been given a new assignment with less than three days' rest from his last one in Morocco. That particular one had involved both Spanish and French intelligence agencies because the one to be extracted was a Moroccan with questionable French citizenship who had managed to tell both agencies that he intended, in any manner possible, to defect to Spain. Since he was unable to leave Morocco legally because he was an Air Force officer assigned to the Western Sahara in El Aaium with its important airport, Langley's clandestine agent was sent there to extract the officer. The agent traveled with a French passport; and with several rounds of baksheesh, he was successful in getting to El Aauim. The trip out of Morocco with the officer — who had been given a French passport by the agent — was difficult and circuitous. They flew from El Aaium to Marrakech; drove from there in a rental car to Casablanca; took a bus from there to Tangier; and flew from there to Madrid. After handing over the Moroccan to the station chief in the American embassy who would debrief him prior to releasing him to the Spanish authorities, the agent was told to remain in Madrid for a briefing on his next assignment in three days.

He was told in his subsequent briefing that intelligence

indicated that a Soviet naval officer assigned to the nuclear submarine fleet had managed to defect in Helsinki during a friendly meeting between the Finnish and Soviet naval commands. He had, over several weeks, made his way to Stockholm where he was wounded by Soviet agents in an aborted mission to capture the officer. He was rescued and treated by Swedish peace activists who slowly smuggled him over a period of several weeks to Helsingborg. He was still recovering from his gunshot wound during this slow and careful journey. A few Danish citizens waited for him and his Swedish helpers as they crossed the narrow inlet to Helsinger in Denmark. The naval officer was taken from there to a safe house in Copenhagen where he remained for eight days before he was moved to the small Danish island of Fehmarn.

The agent was told to fly from Madrid to London and from there to St. Petersburg. He was to ascertain definitely that the high-alert intelligence report concerning a Soviet naval officer from a nuclear submarine had in fact defected. After making sure from trusted informants that the report was correct, he left for Tallinn by train. The distance of about 325 kilometers went quickly and without incidence. When he arrived in the old university town, he took a ferry the next morning to Helsinki via the Tallink Silja Oy. He disembarked from the ferry at the West Terminal 1 where his French passport easily allowed him entry into Finland. He took a local city bus into Helsinki where he went to the American embassy.

He was briefed on the current situation of the Soviet naval officer. He was told the defector was no longer in Finland. He was informed with the highest level of certainty that the officer had been moved successfully to a small Danish island off the coast of Germany. He was asked to fly the next morning from Helsinki to Copenhagen where he would be given a current status report in the American embassy. He was to continue using his French passport.

He was assured in Copenhagen during his briefing by

intelligence which was backed by collaborating Danish intelligence that the Soviet naval officer was still in Danish territory. Denmark's government requested that the American clandestine agent fly from Copenhagen to Hamburg to effect the extraction. The Danes made it clear that they did not want any foreign covert efforts to be made in their territory. The agent could go by train from Hamburg to the Danish island of Fehmarn where the officer was in a safe house in the village of Puttgarden. It was also made clear to him that he was to spend as little time as possible in Danish territory effecting the extraction.

He flew that afternoon from Copenhagen to Hamburg. He went through emigration with no problems. He got a room in a hotel near the Flughafen Hamburg. He took an early train the next morning to the Danish island of Fehmarn. He immediately noticed after boarding the train ferry from Heiligenhafen to Fehmarn an unusual number of males who definitely were not German Hausfrauen going to buy inexpensive butter in Danish territory. He heard snippets of Russian from some of them. This made him both very curious and cautious. His briefing did not include the possibility of Soviet — or east German for that matter — agents going to the small Danish island. He knew that Hamburg in general had a large number of foreign agents who had various assignments none of which were overt.

After disembarking from the train ferry, he watched where the ones whom he thought were foreign agents dispersed. Most left in groups of two in various directions. All attempted to act nonchalant as though they were on a day trip. He saw that some remained near the harbor as though they were waiting for the next train ferry. Some began walking around the little village looking at the few shops. A few began walking the 10 or so kilometers to Puttgarden which was where the naval officer was being hidden. Two of them got on the local bus with the agent to travel to Puttgarden. He had now seen 11 of the very suspicious men. He knew that the USSR was very serious about capturing the defected naval officer. He would have to be extremely aware of his surroundings now that he had identified agents whom he highly suspected were Soviet agents.

Upon arriving at the small bus station in Puttgarden, he walked slowly to the safe house where the defector had been placed. He made absolutely certain that he was not being followed. He rang the doorbell at the little house; and when the door was opened enough for him to see the person opening it, he asked the question identifying himself as an agent. He received the correct answer from the Dane who had a large and bloody bandage on his forehead. The agent noticed at once that the room he entered had very obviously been ransacked. The injured Dane told him that three men whom he could only identify as foreign had burst in during the early morning around 3:00 a.m. They said nothing as they beat him and thoroughly searched the small house.

The Dane told the agent that his two German shepherd dogs had alerted him to possible intruders. As the three men were breaking into his house, he had the Soviet naval officer — who had barely recovered from his wound — go to the cellar in the backyard. He also let his two watchdogs out into the backyard where their ferocious snarling would likely deter any of the three intruders from going there. They tore the house apart looking for the defector. One of the men beat the Dane on his forehead and left cheek with his pistol. As the Dane hoped, they did not go outside. They finally left with a dire warning that they might return. They said, with a heavy Slavic accent, that they will find the traitor to our Motherland.

The agent left the house quickly in order not to be spotted by anyone. He told the Dane to move the defector as soon as possible to another house far from his. The Soviet naval officer was moved with the assistance of the agent to a new safe house by 7:00 a.m. He was informed that someone whom he could explicitly trust would come to his new place of hiding before noon tomorrow. The officer asked no questions but was quite obviously relieved to hear that. He was also told the man appearing tomorrow would assist him in getting to West Germany. He was finally told to speak only German and that he would be given a valid German passport.

The agent left Fehmarn on the afternoon train ferry back to Hamburg. There were several recognizable foreign agents also on the train ferry. This did not surprise him; at the very least, he would now be able to identify some of them. He did not like having to make a second trip back to Puttgarden because of the very real possibility of being recognized and therefore closely followed when he returned. He observed closely those on the train ferry whom he suspected were foreign agents. They were experienced because they remained silent thus avoiding speaking Russian or German. When the train ferry docked at Heiligenhafen, he waited until all the passengers had disembarked before he left. He noticed from the deck that the agents left in pairs in different directions.

He went to the American consulate in Hamburg where he explained to the station chief the changed situation concerning the one to be extracted. He emphasized that there was little guarantee that the second safe house where the Soviet naval officer had been moved would not have been compromised. He told the station chief that he would have to be armed on his second trip. He was given a non-magazined Luger with a silencer and told that the use of it was to be his decision. He understood that he had to avoid terminating any Soviet agents if at all possible. It was explained to him that two high-level men from Langley would be present in the consulate tomorrow to debrief the officer. This comment could only mean that Langley fully expected the extraction to be successful.

He left early the next morning on the ferry train from Hamburg back to the Danish island of Fehmarn. He had with him the valid German passport for the one to be extracted.

He noticed at once that, in addition to the German housewives going to Denmark to purchase inexpensive butter, there were two foreign agents also going to the Danish island. They would have other business in mind than buying butter. He would watch them closely during the trip and also where they went after arriving on Fehmarn. If they took the only bus to Puttgarden, there could be only one reason: they were looking for the defector.

After arriving on the island, he walked around the small port town being cautious as he observed the two foreign agents. They went into a small cafe' to get coffee. When he saw that they would miss the first bus to Puttgarden, he got on the bus. He immediately realized that the two who did not get on the fist bus would be reinforcements for the one whom he remembered who did not return yesterday. There was little doubt that the remaining one would have located the second safe house where the naval officer had been moved. That one would meet the other two and lead them to the house fully expecting to capture the defector and take him back to the USSR where he would be tried as a traitor with an immediate execution following a show trial.

As he walked to the new safe house, he hoped he would be able to see the Soviet agent who had remained in Puttgarden overnight. When he was within 20 meters of the house, he saw a man standing near a house next to the safe house holding a pistol. He was so intent on watching the door of the house that he did not see the agent approaching. The agent terminated him with a head shot.

He quickly entered the house and found the Soviet naval officer lying in obvious pain from his wound which had reopened when he was moved the previous day. The Dane, who owned the house, told the agent that he had changed the bandages and also given him some antibiotics. The agent asked him in Russian if he would be able to make the trip to Hamburg. As the officer was answering, the two Soviet agents whom the agent had earlier identified burst into the house. They had looks of total surprise on their faces when they saw the agent in the same room as the defector they were looking for. Before they could open their jackets to get their weapons, their surprised looks were made permanent by the heavy slugs from the agent's Luger entering their foreheads.

He carefully assisted the officer out of the house into the Dane's car. Instead of taking the bus, which would have attracted undue attention, from Puttgarden to the train ferry's dock; he had the Dane to drive them the 10 or so kilometers. This gave the agent enough time to explain to the officer what would occur once they got int the American consulate in Hamburg. As he gave the officer the German passport he was to use, the officer assured him that he would find the necessary strength to make this final and short trip to freedom.

During the uneventful train ferry trip to Heiligenhafen, he explained in detail the sequence of what the officer could expect. He wanted to make sure that this high-level defector was not only comfortable with but also knowledgeable about everything. It was important for him to know that nothing would resemble Soviet-type interrogations and that he would be taken care of. When he told the officer that there would be two men from Langley who would conduct his debriefing in the American consulate, he responded by saying that he had much that he wanted to divulge about the Soviet submarine fleet.

As they were taking a taxi to the American consulate, the officer thanked the agent several times for making it possible for him to live in freedom in the West. Twice the officer began to speak about the submarine fleet and twice the agent had to tell him in no uncertain terms that he not only did not want to hear anything but also that his sole job was to bring him safely to the American consulate in Hamburg. The officer told the agent at the second reprimand that is not what a KBG agent would have said. The officer strongly emphasized that a Soviet agent would have wanted to hear absolutely everything because he would use the information as a leverage in the KBG organization for his personal advancement and, if possible, with the Politburo. He told the agent that he was thankful that what he would disclose would be given only to Langley and not to an individual agent.

After arriving at the American consulate and being escorted into the small office of the station chief, the Soviet naval officer was introduced to the two men from Langley who would, over several days, debrief him. He was assured by the station chief that what he revealed in his debriefing would be of immense importance to American and NATO security.

The officer turned to thank once again the agent who had at personal risk brought him safely to the West and freedom; however, the clandestine agent had already left.

LATE ARRIVAL

When he had been contacted by Langley and told to report in a week; he figured that, because there seemed to be no urgency, his next assignment would be reasonably easy. After his last assignment where, in the end in order to be successful, he had to kill a foreign agent; he was in no mood to repeat that action. He knew thoroughly that all he did was, and had to be, cloaked in complete denials from Langley. This was the only way the American government could not be involved. He accepted this with ease, and after so many years found the subterfuges normal. He realized that when he either retired or resigned from the clandestine operations, he would have burdens few would ever have. He also accepted this as part of what he was and would ultimately be.

There were few countries, both friendly and adversarial, in which he had not had assignments. Most had been what were euphemistically called high risk only because of the degree of difficulty in extracting persons of high value. He had early on in his 13 year career gained the reputation, because he had earned it, of accepting those assignments which inherently presented mental and physical challenges which other agents eschewed. He had always found them both interesting and fulfilling and never difficult in the sense of not being able to accomplish them. This personal Weltanschauung made him well-known to agents friendly and foreign. Almost no one knew him personally, and fewer still recognized him physically. He had no friends because he trusted nobody. These traits served him very well on his assignments. He wanted it no other way.

As a child he was deeply interested and drawn to geography and languages. From collecting stamps and reading atlases constantly, he learned much about the countries in which, many years later, he would be working. He remembered that in the fourth grade he knew the capital of Azerbaiján but his teacher did not. When he was 12 years old, his father bought him a U.S. border patrol Spanish grammar book. He taught himself Spanish before studying it in high school. His undergraduate and graduate degrees were in languages. While at a foreign university on a doctoral fellowship, he studied Russian taught in German. He had always wanted to study a foreign language taught in a language not his native one because of the mental challenges doing so would provide.

As the airplane neared Dulles, he knew he should call his parents explaining that he would be delayed in seeing them once again; however, he also knew he would be unable to do what most took for granted. He often wondered whether he would be as patient and understanding as they should he have a child who was seldom home — or for that matter — in the country. That they never questioned him was a relief. That he could never tell them what he did was a necessary burden he fully accepted. When he had a rare long assignment in a country, he would mail his parents picture postal cards as though he were a tourist. He was never comfortable with doing that because it was a prevarication. He hoped that this next assignment would be done quickly so that he could return to the United States and have some time to visit his parents. Surely the next extraction, he prayed, would not come immediately after this new one. The problem always was, he knew, there were no assurances of that happening.

When the airplane had landed, he retrieved his small roll-on from the overhead bin. He noticed a female foreign national who was observing him. He would have to make certain that she did not follow him outside of the airport. After many years of being aware of who and what were around him, seeing her without her knowing that he memorized everything about her took only a few seconds.

He did not have an American passport with him because he had entered the previous country with a United Kingdom passport which he left at the American embassy of that country. He was given a Canadian passport with correct entry and exit visas of several countries which he had theoretically gone to. Langley always had this sort of thing in proper order. What his name was on any passport did not matter. What mattered was that they were properly documented and accepted, and they always had been.

He presented his Canadian passport to the American immigration officer while exchanging pleasantries, and was duly admitted to the United States. He then rode the train to the baggage area. He had no luggage, but there would be enough noise that he could quickly call his contact at Langley without being overheard. He informed his contact about the female foreign national. His pickup spot was then cancelled. He was told to take two taxis — stopping once and then getting another taxi — to Old Alexandria and go to the restaurant where George Washington had once dined. Redundancy was a needed requirement in his work.

After arriving at the restaurant, he crossed the street and walked 20 or so meters down toward the Potomac. When he was satisfied no one was following him, he returned up the hill; crossed the street at a different location; and went into the restaurant. He ordered a beer and told the waiter that was all he wanted. Soon a man in jeans and a long-sleeved blue shirt approached him and casually asked him when the

Wizards would next play at home. He answered that he was not sure. Those were the correct passwords. The man left and he finished his beer.

When he went outside, he saw the man leaning against a well-used beige Toyota sedan. He walked past the man and car; stopping as though remembering something all the while observing those walking on the sidewalk. He turned and went back to the car and quickly got in the back seat. Neither said a word on the trip to Langley. They went through the highly guarded and secured entrance being recognized as employees. After the man parked the car in the covered garage, he got out and walked to the entrance of the world's supreme intelligence headquarters.

He took the escalator to the next floor where he walked to a bank of elevators. He entered the one on the left and punched floor seven. The other three people on the elevator said nothing to him after they saw which floor he was going to. They got off at floor five. When he exited at floor seven, he saw all that he had been accustomed to from his previous visits: long corridors with guards and a few people walking toward the dining room. He had once had lunch there because of an invitation from an analyst whose expertise was a country in the Middle East. It had been a pleasant and informative hour or so.

He walked to the Director's office door and was let in at once. He was never surprised at how people on this floor knew who was there and had appointments. Security here was paramount. Nobody could get here without both permission and being known. He almost, he thought, had pity on any who would attempt such a foolhardy endeavor.

The Director was sitting on the balcony outside his office with a thick folder lying on the table and holding a sheaf of papers which he was reading intently. He motioned him to sit opposite him at the table. The Director of Clandestine Operations sat at the other end of the table holding a second folder. He knew that this folder would hold papers he would need as well as an outline of the assignment. He also knew this would be gone over minutely. The Director of Logistics would give him details of flights and other matters. She sat at the opposite end of the table from the Director of Clandestine Operations.

The view from the balcony was, as always, impressive. Little wonder the Director came out there as often as he reasonably could. The Director had once told him that, when he worked sitting on the balcony, he was able to focus more clearly on a project than sitting behind his large desk in his office. It helped him, he said, to be free from walls.

The Director informed him at the beginning of their meeting that the agency had an unusual problem. The person of interest had defected from an eastern country; had disappeared for eight months; and had reappeared in a western country where she was living with relatives who had been there for several years. The patriarch of the family, her great uncle, had an import-export company which the agency had been monitoring for some time. He was involved with exporting western items to his former eastern country, and was importing non-consequential items from that country. A few of the exported items were on a watch list for possible end misuse. The Director told him that the agency did not trust the patriarch. During the time she had been living with her relatives, she had not been suspected of being involved with her great uncle's business.

Her mother and father had been imprisoned by the eastern country's authorities from the time she had graduated with a doctorate in mathematics from the state university 11 years ago. She had neither heard from nor seen her parents since their arrest. During the years prior to her defection - which occurred at a conference in another western country - she worked in a state research facility on cybersecurity. She had developed an algorithm which could trace encrypted telephone calls. The intelligence agencies of the West had been apprised thoroughly of this by the clandestine group from a small country friendly to the West.

Complicating an already difficult situation was the bothersome fact that three other western countries coveted having her. Their intelligence people would be working hard to secure her in order that she could apply her expertise in their cybersecurity research. All would be working separately without sharing any information on their plans. Her home country would also be deeply involved in removing her by any means from her present location. The Agency knew that her home country had assigned three of their highly skilled and ruthless agents to extract her. The western country where she was currently living with her relatives had already made several attempts to convince her to work for it. She had refused all of their requests.

The Director gave a terse and factual summation: there would be agents from her home country, agents from Eastern Europe, and agents from the United States all in the same large city involved in her extraction. There likely would be, the Director said, possibly 10 total high - level agents there. Apart from the obvious problems of avoiding the other agents, there was a political matter which was highly important. The President did not want the four western countries to know of the Agency's involvement because of NATO and an impending conference where he wanted to emphasize transparency in their mutual endeavors. The Director concluded, in an understatement, that a successful extraction would not be easy.

The Director of Clandestine Operations then opened his folder and began outlining the details of the project. He began by saying that he understood the so-far silent agent preferred working alone but there would now be an exception. He would this time, because of important appearances, be working with a female agent from the small country which had initially discovered the cybersecurity person, her background, and her work.

They would be given a marriage certificate indicating that they had been married four years after having met in graduate school. They would be given papers showing that both were professors at a large state university where they had earned a sabbatical: she a professor of music and he a professor of literature. She would be writing a book on the music of the Orient at the university in the large city where the person of interest was living. He would be writing a book on the poetry of her country. The targeted person played the violin and had translated some of her country's poetry into English. It was hoped that their research into the music and poetry of her country would afford them, eventually, access to her.

They would have documents indicating that they had lived in an apartment near the state university and had paid rent. Also the apartment in the city where they would be living while doing research had been arranged. The respective departments of music and literature had accepted them to do research based on their resumes which Langley had provided. Finally, they would be given passports of the country where they were professors. The female agent had been given the same documents and briefing.

The Director of Logistics then gave him the not-to-be changed details of their actions and flights. They both would fly separately to the city where they were professors. She would arrive first and meet him a day later at the airport. She would leave within three hours after Langley had informed her intelligence group that the briefing was concluded. They would remain in the city for a week during which time they would make themselves known to their neighbors. They would go at least twice weekly to the university's library. In the event their apartment was compromised, evidence of their individual research was to be found. Entry cards to the library had been arranged.

She would fly from her home country to a country north of their targeted country. She would then take another flight to the city where the person of interest was living. After she had arrived to their apartment without being followed, both intelligence groups would be notified. He would then leave Dulles flying to a country far south of their targeted country. He would take another flight to the city where the female agent already was. She would meet him at the airport having taken a taxi there. They both would take two taxis to their apartment. They would first stop at a small shop to purchase some food, and then take a second taxi to their apartment.

The owner of the little grocery shop would be their only trusted foreign contact in the city. He would provide them with local information. He had been recruited by Langley more than a decade ago. He had a well-established network of informants.

They would, by mutual agreement, report weekly to a clandestine field operative from Langley. They had to report together. Only he would be given the contact information for the American operative. The intelligence group of his companion female agent had at first strenuously objected to this arrangement, but finally agreed to this strict term of Langley. He was to contact the operative solely by a local pay telephone - using a different one each time. A face-to-face meeting was to be done only in a dire situation. The field operative would give them minute details on the transfer of the one to be extracted. Finally, going into either's embassy was to be avoided at all costs.

They were to befriend the porter of their apartment building using small gifts of cigarettes, bags of potatoes, meats, and cheeses during the time they would be there. They were not to recruit him but only gain his confidence as he would see them daily. He made very little money in the job he had kept for many years; so meaningful gifts would not only help him but also the agents. He saw everyone who came and went at the apartment building.

The Director of Logistics concluded by telling him that the

first thing they had to do was change the locks on the door of their apartment. She gave him the name and address of a trusted locksmith. They were to have no landline telephone installed. They were to present themselves to all who saw them as academics on a limited income.

When the three briefings were over, he was told to take the same Agency's car to the shopping mall at Tyson's corner where he would take two taxis to the small apartment near Falls Church which Langley kept for rotating agents. He would remain there until informed that his companion agent was in their apartment in the targeted city. He would then walk several blocks away and take one taxi to Dulles. As usual he was to notice anyone who followed him once he was in the airport.

When he was finally in the sparsely furnished apartment, he wrote a long letter to his parents discussing many things before he told them that another business trip had interfered with his plans to visit them. He wrote, finally, that he would without fail see them as soon as possible. He addressed the envelope without sealing it. When he left for his assignment, an agent would read it and then post it.

All too soon an agent arrived informing him that he could now leave. He left and walked eight blocks before he hailed a taxi to take him to Dulles. He went through security and walked slowly to his departure gate. Not too surprisingly there would not be a full flight since few — even in D.C. — needed to go to this country. He sat in a cramped economy class seat next to a couple who, they said, were missionaries. He told them he was also a Christian and would pray for them. This satisfied them, and they did not speak to him for the entire flight.

When the airplane landed and he had retrieved his small overnight bag from the overhead bin, he went to an exchange bank where he got some currency and several coins. He then went to a pay phone where he called the apartment back in America. An agent answered, and he told the agent that the weather was fine and hung up. Since he had a 90 minute layover, he bought a cup of strong coffee and a large sandwich. As he drank the coffee and slowly ate the sandwich, he instinctually noticed the travelers waiting for the flight to the targeted country. All appeared to be citizens of that country because of their clothing and language.

The next flight was both full and uneventful. When he landed, he went through immigration with ease. He wondered what his companion agent would look like. He saw several females obviously waiting for specific passengers but none who approached him. Soon he saw a tall and slender woman with dark hair waving exuberantly at him as though she were happy to see him. He waved back and went up to her. She hugged him and told him they were supposed to be married and for him to act accordingly. He was surprised at her lack of an English accent. He took her hand and they walked out to the taxi stand talking animately.

They got into a taxi and she gave the driver the address of the small grocery shop. She told the driver that they needed to buy some food and that her husband had been gone for several days. She spoke so convincingly that the driver replied in broken English that he understood the need to buy food — and jokingly that there were no doubt other needs. She laughed at the last comment.

When they arrived at the grocery shop, they saw that it was crowded. They had to pretend they were looking for many items before they could give the owner the safely-arrived password. The owner must have guessed who they were because he waited until most of the shoppers had left. The female agent asked him if he had any meat. The owner recognized the password and visibly relaxed. As he helped them by wrapping the cheese they purchased, he casually told them that he had the usual shoppers. He also told them he hoped they would return. If anyone were eavesdropping, he or she would have heard only a shop owner welcoming new customers.

She paid for their purchases; both told the owner they would definitely return; and he and she went outside and got into a taxi. Once again she gave the taxi driver the address where they were going in faultless language. The driver asked if they were instructors at the university. He explained his question by telling them that the apartment building was near the university. Many people from the university had apartments in the building. Both recognized this as an important piece of information. She told the driver they both were at the university as guests doing research.

When they arrived at the apartment building, she paid the driver and thanked him. They took their bags of groceries and his small overnight bag to the two wide front doors of their apartment building. After ringing the bell, an older but sturdy man opened one of the doors. He was the porter who lived in a very small apartment next to the front doors. The female agent introduced her husband to the porter telling him that he had just arrived. They gave him a few oranges, some slices of ham, and a loaf of bread. He thanked them profusely as he took them up the stairs to their second floor apartment.

As they entered the apartment, he noticed that she had arranged the chairs in the sitting room in such a way that none would be visible from the sidewalk across the street. She had even pushed the small dining table up against a wall so that nobody sitting there could be seen from the outside. The tiny kitchen had a small window looking out to an unused courtyard. She was good he thought, and that relieved him.

When they unpacked their groceries to put them away, they found a brief but quite complete note from the grocer outlining who were repeat shoppers; how many new shoppers came in the past week; and how many foreigners had shopped in his store. After both had read and memorized the contents of the note, she tore it in to many small pieces and placed those along with two or three sections of an orange in a damp paper napkin and flushed all easily down the toilet. She had been well trained he thought.

The next morning he walked to the locksmith and made arrangements for their lock to be changed late that afternoon. When he entered the apartment building, he gave the porter a pack of cigarettes. He knew that few residents of the building paid any attention to the porter much less gave him small gifts. He knew also that sooner or later these gestures would pay off. The porter saw everyone who came into and left the building; so he would notice strangers coming in. All had to receive his permission to go up the stairs.

They agreed that when the locksmith arrived, one would remain in the apartment and the other would go down and stand outside on the opposite sidewalk. Locksmiths in this part of the world did not have sterling reputations; so one of them would watch his work in the apartment and the other one would see whether or not anyone came with the locksmith. This part of their work was petty but necessary. Those who ignored the small things often paid dearly when the large matters would appear.

After the locksmith had changed the two locks on the door to their apartment and had given her correct and working keys, he left with a small parcel containing some cheese and salami from them as a well-meant thank you. When the locksmith exited the building, he did not notice the agent leaning against a poplar tree four spaces from his parked van. He drove slowly away in his smoking old work van. The agent then quickly looked up and down the street; crossed it; and went into the building. He told the porter that he did not have to walk up the stairs with him. The porter seemed happy to hear that.

He knocked once and then waited a second or two and then knocked three times in rapid succession. They had agreed on this method of identification. She opened the door and gave him the two new keys. They had discussed that they would alternate possession of the two keys each time they left their apartment. This provided a layer of security which they might need.

The next morning they walked to the library in order to observe activity on the streets and sidewalks as well as to see who was looking in the shop windows. They also wanted to notice if anyone followed them from their apartment. Their walk to the library was uneventful and pleasant. They walked slowly talking as a married couple might. They wanted to present a picture of normalcy in the event they were being observed.

The entrance of the large library was crowded with students and faculty members both sitting and standing in the sun before they had to go in to begin their morning's reading and research. The large number of people afforded the two agents a welcome opportunity to see if any in the crowd did not appear to be from the university. There were three people whom they noticed who did not appear to be either students or faculty. They had neither briefcases or backpacks, and were standing near the entrance of the library looking at those entering. They also did not appear to the two agents that they were associated with one another. This could mean they were agents from three separate intelligence groups. They would have to be watched.

The two agents presented their library entry cards which were validated at once. They were shown the very large reading room where they could take their research material to read. They were also told how to request books and articles from the archival stacks. They, as everyone with library cards, were allowed to browse through the open stacks. They placed their briefcases on one of the long tables and went to their respective research stacks: she for music and he for literature.

They spent several hours moving through the enormous library acquainting themselves with floor plans, exits, and librarians. They each made it a point to speak to others doing readings and research. This would be repeated each time they went to the library. It was very important that they were recognized as persons doing research and nothing else.

They had at the beginning of the morning agreed to meet at the bulletin board area in the lobby at a certain time. They saw a notice for a concert in the evening in two day's time. The concert featured a violinist from the targeted person's country playing a Stradivarius. They both knew, and discussed this as they walked back to their apartment, that the targeted person would attend the concert. They agreed that it would be best if they arrived at the concert hall a few minutes apart and then sit in two different sections. These actions would allow them to notice separately those arriving and those sitting near them.

They stopped at the little grocery shop to buy two loaves of bread, cheese, and some sliced meat. They told the owner that they would be going to the concert. He in turn told them that it was a much-anticipated event. His informants had told him that several foreign agents would likely be attending. He also told them that, so far, they were known only as a foreign couple doing research. This was welcome news.

The porter at their apartment building told them, as they gave him a loaf of bread and some of the sliced meat, that two strangers had come to the building while they were out asking if there were any recent move-ins. They claimed they were from the local government taking a census of newly arrived people. They casually thanked him for the news, and told him they hoped he would enjoy the bread and meat. They then went up to their apartment.

When they were safely inside, they discussed the five probable foreign agents: three in the library and now two at their apartment building. They were satisfied, however, that none of those suspected them. If there were, as the Director had told him in the briefing, likely ten high-level agents all working to extract the person of interest, they had now identified possibly five of them. They quickly reasoned that the other five would very possibly be at the concert.

They decided that they should — together as required — contact Langley's clandestine field operative in order to report their initial observations. Before they left their apartment to walk to a pay telephone, they looked out of the only window which faced the street in their apartment. They saw a woman slowly riding a bicycle on the sidewalk opposite their building. She was very carefully looking at the building. Since none of the other five were woman, they surmised that she would have to be the sixth agent. They waited until she had gone on out of their sight before they left the building. They told the porter that they were going for a late afternoon walk. Once outside the building, they crossed the street to the sidewalk where the woman had been riding. When they saw she was nowhere in sight, they walked to the second pay telephone booth from where they were.

He called the U.S. clandestine field operative; gave his password; and received the correct password in turn. He told the field operative that they had potentially identified six agents out of the probable ten. He told the agent that the last one was a female. There was a slight pause before the agent told him that she was one of the highest ranking agents from the target's home country. There was then a longer pause. The agent told him that she would be armed with a silenced weapon and would never hesitate to use it. The agent then hung up.

As they walked back to their apartment, they discussed what they should do and how it should be done concerning the foreign agents. The concert would be in the evening two days from now. They knew they had to identify the remaining four foreign agents. The concert would be given in the large hall located across a plaza from the library and parallel on the same street to the multi-storied classroom building. They knew there would be many places the foreign agents could, at a minimum, blend into the crowds of students, faculty, and townspeople the evening of the concert. They decided that each of the two remaining days and two nights — counting today — would be spent at the library as usual but also include a thorough reconnaissance of the concert hall's adjoining rooms with all the exits noted as well as the ground level rooms of the classroom building. Too many places to look in too little time confronted them.

That evening in their apartment they discussed what they should do each of the remaining days and, more importantly, the night of the concert. Each would purchase a ticket a day apart so that it would make certain they were seated in different sections of the hall. They reasoned that the targeted person and likely her great-uncle and perhaps other relatives would take a train in from the suburbs rather than driving his car or taking a bus or taxi. It was a risk they might miss her at the train station which was less than a kilometer from the concert hall. They knew from briefings that the target and her great-uncle would walk rather than take a taxi or bus from the train station. They further believed the foreign agents would very likely be focused on bus transportation since several lines stopped at the plaza where the concert hall and classroom building were. She would be at the train station 90 minutes prior to the start of the concert, and he would be at the area where the bus stops were. They would meet after the concert in a cafe' near the plaza.

They went to the library the next morning as usual so anyone who might suspect them would soon believe they were merely researchers. The only deviation was that they went into the concert hall to learn where all exits and restrooms were. It was rather straight forward with no observed problems inside the hall itself. The large concert auditorium had a sweeping balcony with several hundred seats on the main floor. The auditorium could possibly present a few problems. She purchased her balcony seat at the ticket office before they left.

The following morning — the day of the evening concert — they first went to the classroom building and carefully checked out the ground floor. There were too many places someone could hide on that floor. They decided that the other agents would also find the same problem and not place a large emphasis on the building.

As the walked to the library from the classroom building, they discussed when they would leave their apartment and where they would find each other after the concert ended if the small cafe' was too crowded. She would have a seat in the balcony, and he would have a seat in the back of the auditorium. It was vitally important that they arrived together. She would have to walk from the train station back to the concert hall; so he would wait at the bus stop area for a while before he walked over to the hall to meet her. The timing of the meeting was somewhat tricky but manageable.

After their usual time in the library, they left and began walking back to their apartment. Near the front of the library were a man and woman whom they had not seen before. Both of them were scanning the people going into and leaving the library. They were not faculty or students judging from their behaviors and clothing. They remained there without moving; so the two agents knew the man and woman were very likely two more foreign agents.

As they left the area of the library, they were satisfied that the two foreign agents had not noticed them; and more importantly, they were not being followed. They went over again their plans for the evening. They knew that the difficult part would be meeting at the concert hall after she had walked from the train station following, they hoped, the targeted person and whomever of her relatives who might be with her.

They walked slowly to the ticket office of the concert hall where they purchased a seat for him in the back of the auditorium. They would be able to observe the entrance of the targeted person from their two vantage points. They believed also that by her walking to the train station and his waiting at the bus stop area prior to the concert would allow them to notice how the targeted person would arrive. One of them would follow her, and likely her relative, to the concert hall. As they had discussed earlier, this would be the difficult part as far as timing was concerned. They also had decided that she would approach the targeted person at intermission while he would be standing a few meters away. She would engage the woman in a conversation about the concert which featured music from the target's country. She would also attempt — given time — to explain that she was doing research in the music of the country. He would be observing others who might be watching or approaching the target.

As they neared the grocery store, they saw three police cars in front of it. There was also an animated crowd on the sidewalk. They learned quickly that the owner had been kidnapped by two foreigners. His wife had been severely beaten by them. They knew they had to call the U.S. clandestine field operative to apprise him of this disturbing turn of events.

They walked toward their apartment where they noticed a car, which they had never seen before, parked near the apartment building with two people in it. They continued walking past the vehicle and crossed at the next intersection to the other sidewalk. They walked to a pay telephone booth where he called the operative; gave his password; and received the correct password in turn. He told the operative tersely about the kidnapping and the strange can near their apartment. The operative told him that they might be compromised and that several foreign agents had suspected the grocer was an informant. He also said their apartment building was apparently on a watch list. He concluded by telling him that all suspected foreign agents would be at the concert with some going early to the train station and some at the bus stop area. The agent then hung up.

They now knew that the evening of the concert would be the time for them to execute the extraction. They also knew that all the foreign agents would be at the concert with some outside near the bus stop and perhaps one at the train station. They had to coordinate their movements and trust fully the other when they separated at the concert hall.

Two hours prior to the concert, they left their apartment and called the clandestine field operative with the correct passwords being exchanged. He gave them the minute details on the transfer of the targeted person as he had been told he would receive during his briefing at Langley. There would be two white four door sedans: one parked 50 meters from the train station and one 50 meters from the bus stop near the concert hall. They were to approach the targeted person carefully keeping in mind that she likely would be with her great uncle. They were to tell them quickly but clearly that they were here to help them escape to the United States. Using force, they were told, to place them in the vehicle would be a last resort. The drivers of the white sedans knew where to take the passengers. There were given instructions in how to vacate their apartment and leave the country.

They left the telephone booth and began walking to the concert hall. The sidewalks were teeming with people; this made it easy for them to walk without being noticed. It also made it difficult for them to observe any person who looked or acted out of the ordinary. When they get to the bus stop, he remained there and she began walking toward the train station. They had agreed to meet back at the concert hall just prior to the beginning of the concert.

While he was at the bus stop, he pretended he was waiting for someone to join him all the while looking for those who might be foreign agents. He saw four whom he believed were agents. They loitered outside and finally went into the concert hall.

Fifteen minutes after the concert had begun, his fellow agent had not yet returned to meet him. He began walking toward the train station to see what was causing her delay. Though he trusted her training, he knew that many things could have caused her to improvise at the moment of the targeted person's arrival.

As he approached the train station, he saw one of the white sedans going down the street in the opposite direction of the concert hall. He noticed that an older man and woman were in the back seat. Finally, he saw his companion walking toward him.

She told him that she had stood behind one of the large pillars outside the train station waiting for the arrival of their target. When the target emerged from the station, she saw that she was accompanied by not only her great-uncle but also by the dangerous female foreign agent. She told him that she waited until the three had just passed the pillar where she was hiding. She then hit the agent hard across the back of her neck which caused the agent to fall at once totally unconscious. She told the targeted person and her great-uncle that she was here to take them safely to freedom. She put them in the white sedan without any hesitation or problem from them.

They walked slowly back toward the concert hall; past the library; past the grocery store; and into their apartment building. They went into their apartment; packed their few belongings; and left.

NEAR THE LAKE

He had been slightly injured in Kenya on his assignment there. It was nothing serious; however, he had wanted to go to Zanzibar to rest and heal but was unable to do so. It had been a difficult extraction with far too many contradictions from both informants and government officials. To make a complicated extraction even more worse, nobody seemed to trust or understand the ones involved. What should have taken less than three weeks to accomplish took almost a month. When the two subjects were finally extracted and safely out of the country, he went to the American embassy to give his debriefing. It was there that he told the station chief that he wanted a few days off in order to travel to Zanzibar to rest. He was told no. He was to fly immediately from Nairobi to Khartoum to be briefed on his next assignment.

As he flew to Khartoum, he had a feeling that what he would be told by the station chief in the American embassy there would not be overly pleasant. Every time in his many years as a clandestine agent that he had been requested to go somewhere immediately, the assignments he had been given were circumscribed by time. Extractions were never easy; it was just that some were particularly difficult physically, mentally, and even politically. He never had a choice, given his years of experience and expertise, to refuse accepting an extraction assignment. Langley trusted that he would not only memorize the overall details of what he had to do but also believed explicitly that he would have the required abilities to accomplish the given task. Many promising agents learned quickly that the stress-filled requirements were too onerous for them to continue as clandestine field agents. Only those gifted with extraordinary physical and mental abilities were successful.

When he arrived at the American embassy in Khartoum, he was ushered quickly to the office of the station chief. The agent knew by the book on the chief's face that the briefing would be outlined with demands and the concomitant difficulties needed for his new extraction assignment. He would, as usual, listen intently without asking questions. He preferred to concentrate on what was being said rather than interjecting his questions or comments. He had learned over the years that any briefing he was given — whether at Langley or in an American embassy — was devoid of misunderstandings, or worse, mistakes if he simply listened. Any adjustments would be made in the field not in a briefing.

The station chief did not offer any apologies for the unusual assignment. He explained to the agent that the ones to be extracted were under severe threat of being executed if they could be found by the government. They were currently in hiding approximately 100 kilometers from where the agent would be inserted. His assignment was to locate them; move them to a safe house about 50 kilometers from the city where he would work from; and securely extract them from the country. He would find and meet a local businessman who would provide him with much-needed assistance. All three of the ones to be extracted had previously been arrested and tortured. The man was an intellectual who had written many articles criticizing the repressive regime. He had also given several very public speeches on the same subject. What made him a valued asset to be extracted was that his brother-in-law was a trusted member of the military's inner circle. His knowledge of foreign influence on the military would be very valuable to western countries' intelligence. His wife was a professor in the faculty of fine arts; and since she was the sister of the man in the military's establishment, she was by default highly suspected by the authoritarian ruler. Their 18 year old son had lost his left eye while being tortured. The agent had to get them to the city's harbor and place them on the businessman's commercial boat which would take them to Port Said. There they would be transferred to an American cargo ship which would take them to Haifa. He had five days to accomplish these objectives. The station chief shook his hand and gave him an unusual apology by telling him that he personally was upset with the time constraint placed on this assignment.

Before the agent left the briefing room, he was given a highly classified report from Langley detailing the current situation in the country where he would be inserted. The country's ruler was infuriated by the spread of dissidence in the country. He had ordered mass arrests of intellectuals and anyone associated with them. It was a brutal authoritarian rule with draconian measures employed throughout the country. There was cruel treatment of the country's populace by the hated and feared secret police who permeated the country. The country was in desperate poverty with essential imports always being late in getting to the shops. The regime ruled only by the consent of the armed forces. The American President and his Secretary of State had met with the ruler with few tangible results.

He spent the night after his briefing in Khartoum in a small hotel perhaps 15 kilometers from the airport to which he took an old diesel car which served as a taxi. The embassy had secured for him the ticket from the capital of the Sudan to the capital of his target country. Though he knew the flight would be full, it would at least be an early morning flight. This would give him not only an opportunity to observe who was going to the capital city but also give him ample time to locate the small and old hotel where he was to stay. The boarding area was, as he suspected, crowded with both citizens of the Sudan and many foreigners queuing for passage. He noticed at once that there were several military people in uniform from his targeted country boarding the flight. The flight was uneventful given that the airplane was clearly several decades old. The passenger sitting next to him was a local businessman who told him that where they were going lacked many needed goods and that he hoped to be able to secure several lucrative contracts. He told the agent that the only problem he would face would be receiving permission form the head of external procurements who was a hard-nosed colonel in the armed services who had no regard for the needs of the citizens. He explained to the agent that the military kept some of the approved goods for themselves and sold the rest at inflated prices to government-run stores. He also said that what he sold to the military would have to be barely above what he had paid for the goods.

When he landed, he and all the passengers on the flight were commanded by the authorities at the airport to wait in a large room which was heavily populated by who could only be secret police. The room had little ventilation; was dusty and hot; was filled with flies; and was noisy. The passengers were allowed one at a time to have their papers examined and luggage searched. The only thing which seemed to have any semblance to order were the tight-lipped and profusely sweating immigration officers — all else was a scene of pure chaos with shoving, shouting, and tired passengers. The government quite apparently had no qualms with this being the reception for people arriving from western countries much less from third world countries.

When it was his turn with an immigration officer, he was closely accompanied by a secret policeman only because he was one of three obviously Europeans on the flight. This indicated to him the probability of difficulties for this assignment. Any government which was basically paranoid about those who were not citizens and who were arriving from another third world country would be able to keep tabs on foreigners. He knew that he would have to be vary circumspect in both his movements and meetings. As he was considering these restrictions, he was finally asked to present his passport. When the immigration officer saw it was a Canadian one with stamped visas from Kenya and the Sudan, the officer at once wanted to know what he had been doing in those countries and why he was now in Egypt. The agent was not surprised at the questions considering the political situation in the country.

He told the officer that he had been in Kenya and the Sudan to conduct business for the firm he worked for. He would be doing the same in Egypt. He gave the immigration officer one of his business cards which he guessed the man could not read because it was in English; however, he knew for certain that it would be given to the secret police. On the card was the name, address, and telephone numbers of the company he worked for: Canadian Trans-World Trading. It was a sham firm Langley had had set up; the telephones would be answered; any mail received would be correctly responded to. He was finally given his business visa after a few more questions.

He took a taxi with one other man to the train station which he found was not only exceedingly crowded but also without any apparent order. He found a ticket booth where he bought a general ticket to Alexandria. It meant he would be in an open carriage with natives going to the port city. He did not purchase a so-called first class ticket since it could have brought attention to him. Instead he would be riding with passengers who would be ordinary Egyptians who likely might be complaining about the ruthless regime. He could at least eavesdrop on conversations during the journey. He was not at all surprised to see military officers boarding the more comfortable first class carriages. He also was, in some sense, glad that many secret police were sitting among the poor in not only his carriage but also in all the other general class carriages. He would be able to observe any interaction between the secret police personnel and the oppressed-looking ordinary people.

The trip was hot, noisy, and dusty. All the windows in his carriage had been opened to let in refreshing but hot breezes. Many of the Egyptians on the train were going to visit relatives in Alexandria. Some were hopeful they might find any kind of work in the city since there was none in the villages they had left. All of them attempted strenuously to avoid speaking to the secret police. They did not want to be questioned on the train and then be detained without reason at the end of the trip. One little boy had accidentally touched the revolver of a secret policeman and was slapped across the face so hard that he fell down. The parents could not retaliate in any manner; so all they could do was to comfort their son with downcast faces. He knew this type of oppression would be common.

He got off the train in the western part of Alexandria at the Moharam Bek station. He noticed that the first class carriages emptied at the Mahuttat Misr station. All of the uniformed military men got off there. Most of the Egyptians in his carriage began walking after they disembarked; very few were met by relatives with cars. He also noticed that the secret police mingled with the large number of passengers on the platform — they wanted to see who met whom. One family was stopped and questioned for several minutes before being allowed to leave the station. Every passenger attempted to avoid the secret police; they knew all too well the absolute power the secret police had been given by the regime. There were far too many stories of people being detained never to be seen again for them to risk doing or saying anything which would draw attention to them.

The neighborhood where he got off was very much a poor

part of the city where crowds of people were almost overwhelming. There were scores of small shops selling everything from pots and pans to sandals. Some shops sold green onions, feta cheese, and bread cheaply for workers. The noise in the immediate area of the Moharam Bek neighborhood seemed never to cease. Drivers of donkey carts carrying various goods to shops and needing space to go through the crowds were shouting loudly. Those shouts intermingled with the loud voices of both merchants and people shopping.

While walking through the area, he noticed that there seemed to be some meat but little in the way of other goods such as toilet paper. There were sacks of rice stamped "Gift from the People of The United States of America" openly displayed from which government shops sold. This should have been prohibited but was not. The regime eagerly accepted cargo ships from the USA carrying essential goods for the populace, but had no qualms in selling what should have been given to the Egyptians.

As he walked through Moharam Bek, he quickly noticed that he, being a Nasrani— foreigner—was followed closely by two secret police. He knew at some point on his walk to the very low cost hotel Langley had identified for him that he would be stopped and questioned until they were satisfied with his answers. He hoped they would stop him prior to his arriving at the hotel. He did not want attention drawn to where he would be staying. Since it was a crowded neighborhood with shops everywhere, the secret police — believing his presence here in a poor neighborhood was suspicious — finally stopped him. They wanted to see his identification papers which they scrutinized closely for several minutes before they demanded from him the reasons why he was here. He told them that he had intended to get off at the Mahuttat Misr station, the main train station, but that he had made a mistake and ended up getting off at the Moharam Bek station. He also explained to them that he was in Alexandria on a business trip and that the visa in his passport proved that. After a few more minutes of brusque questions, they let him go.

He walked slowly through the neighborhood so that he could observe shop keepers, local citizens, and the seemingly omnipresent secret police. The secret police had no qualms whatsoever in stopping shoppers and demanding at once answers of their questions. He saw no shopkeepers or citizens greeting them. His walk took perhaps an hour, but it was informative with nuanced knowledge he gained from his observations. He stopped at one shop to buy some feta cheese, green unions, and bread. These would be his filling and delicious dinner. The shopkeeper, who spoke some English, welcomed him to Egypt and to Alexandria in particular.

He found the run-down hotel where Langley wanted him to stay for one night. The owner had been recruited by the Agency many years ago, and was an excellent source for low-level intelligence concerning the mood of poor people. He had never been suspected by the regime of anything anti-government. As he was checking the agent in by carefully writing his name and passport number into his tattered registry book, he invited in Arabic the agent to his room behind the front desk for gahwa - coffee. He told the hotel owner he had the makings of a small meal he would share with him. As they drank the strong and hot coffee and ate the simple meal, the hotel owner told him that the poor people in this neighborhood had little money; few were employed; and the majority believed the regime was not only very repressive but also cared only for the military and people in the upper reaches of the government. He told the agent that many had been arrested and tortured. Some families had not heard from their loved ones who had been arrested for many months.

He went to his small room after the meal where he noticed the obligatory framed photo of the dictator on the wall. After making certain there were no listening devices anywhere in the room, he went to sleep in spite of the noise outside his window. When he awoke early the following morning, the noise from crowds of people seemed never to have ceased. He thanked the hotel's owner and went outside to get a taxi to take him to the Ramla Tram Station. He would meet there a business owner who had good information concerning the ones to be extracted. He waved down a taxi after several minutes of waiting. There were two brothers from Assuit already in the taxi. They owned a business in their home town and were in Alexandria in order to sell what they manufactured to local resellers. They told the agent that the regime paid them far below the market price for their goods. The only way they could make any profit was to sell their products here in Alexandria. They both hoped the regime would not confiscate their plant. Only because they were Coptic Christians, they felt that the regime could at any time and for any reason retaliate against them. When they arrived at the Ramla tram station, the two brothers quickly left the taxi because they did not want to be seen in public with a foreigner.

 He walked from the very crowded tram station toward the cafe where Langley had told him the businessman always had a mid-morning coffee all the while observing those around him. This part of the city was definitely better in appearance than the one he had just left. The noise and crowds, however, were still prevalent. The area around the tram station was filled with young students, university students, and what appeared to be professional people going to their jobs. The secret police mingled among the crowds arriving at and leaving from the Ramla station. They would occasionally stop a group of older students in a very obvious attempt to intimidate them. He noticed that the students answered as sparingly as possible. He overheard one of the secret police asking a student where he father worked. The student would, no doubt, tell her parents when all were home in the late afternoon.

 He found the bustling cafe' and the businessman sitting having his mid-morning coffee. Langley had long wanted a trusted and constant source of information concerning the military of the regime, and this source was finally found in the businessman. His pregnant wife had been killed in a traffic accident involving a speeding military vehicle. Rather than quitting selling various imported goods to the military because of his wife's and unborn child's deaths, he decided he would extract a life-long revenge from the abhorred military. On one of his usual trips to Cairo, he went to the American embassy where, after he spoke of the deaths caused by negligence from the military, he was escorted to the office of Langley's station chief. He agreed that he would supply any intelligence he would learn from his contacts with the military. He also agreed that he would gladly work with Langley in any helpful capacity. He became the most trusted native source of information about the military in Egypt.

The agent explained to the businessman who and what the current situation involved. He was not surprised when the businessman told him he knew the family because of the wife's brother being a member of the military's elite. He told the agent that the family had left Alexandria and were staying with the wife's family in Tanta where, for the time being, they were reasonably safe. Since Tanta was about 100 kilometers from Alexandria, it was not considered a place of anti-regime movements by the secret police. The family had been harassed daily by the secret police; and when they left Alexandria, they took with them very few possessions.

The businessman explained in detail how he would assist not only the family but also the agent in the extraction. He told the agent that he had a small cabin near Lake Idku which was approximately 50 kilometers from Alexandria. Since he often went there to fish in the brackish water, there would be no suspicion concerning the use of his cabin. He told the agent that he would use his large commercial boat in assisting the family to leave the country.

The next day the agent took a tram early to the bus station.

He bought a ticket on what was called the agricultural bus which served the villages and small towns south of Alexandria. He was stopped and questioned for a few minutes by a secret policeman prior to being allowed to board the greatly overcrowded bus. After arriving in Tanta some two hours later, he was thankful the businessman had given him precise directions to the house where the ones to be extracted were staying. It was a small but well-kept house. He was also glad the businessman had told the family that a westerner would be visiting them with good news; nevertheless, both families were frightened and very wary of him. After he explained to them the sequence of what would occur, they relaxed visibly and invited him for lunch of foul mesdames, bread, and hot sweet black tea.

He explained to both families carefully what would happen and how it would be accomplished. A car supplied by the businessman — whom they knew and trusted — would arrive early at their house in two days. They were to take only one suitcase of their belongings. They were to wear the oldest clothes they had in order not to draw any attention to themselves. They would be driven to a cabin near the lake east of Alexandria where they would remain until very early the next day when the agent would arrive at the cabin in an old work van.

When he left before dawn driving from Alexandria to the cabin near Lake Idku, he and dozens of other drivers going to work in the fisheries along the lake were stopped by the secret police at a well-manned roadblock. When it was his turn, he showed the police his business visa. He explained to them that he was going to pick up his workers in order that he could get a load of fish to take to Alexandria's market. After several tense minutes of questioning him and searching the van, he was told to drive on.

He met the three members of the family to be extracted in the cabin near the lake where they had remained inside where they could not be observed. He noticed that they were wearing old clothes which meant they had listened to his earlier instructions. He prefaced his instructions this time with a caution that perhaps the plans he was about to outline might have to be changed ii actions by the secret police warranted any change. He wanted them to understand clearly that minute details of their extraction had been planned with an ultimate success as an end result, but that any unforeseen events in the steps of their extraction would force him to make immediate changes.

He told them that they would drive the van with them to the harbor. There they would unload the van of its cargo to the commercial boat of the businessman. He would take the last crate of fish onto the boat. They were to remain below deck and not to reappear. The boat would take them to Port Said where they would transfer to an American cargo ship. They and he would remain on the ship until it docked at Haifa. They would all fly from there to London. He emphasized that these were the outlines of plans which might go exactly as hoped. All understood the risks involved.

He had driven perhaps 15 kilometers from the cabin when all traffic on the road to the port was halted by the secret police. They questioned each driver and any occupants closely and also checked carefully internal papers. His Canadian passport with a business visa satisfied his questioners. He was allowed to drive on to the harbor with the members of the family.

He parked the van with the ones to be extracted as closely as he could to the docked commercial boat of the business man. All cargoes intended for export were carefully monitored by the port officials. He explained that the crates of fish from Lake Idku were going to Port Said. He showed the officials the paperwork which showed his cargo had been purchased by an American cargo shop. Even after this evidence, he and the three family members — who he explained were his hired workers — were questioned many times by the secret police who appeared to have more authority than the port officials.

This made it difficult for the ones to be extracted to board and remain on the boat.

He told them to go below the deck, and he would bring onboard the last crate of fish. He explained to the secret police that his workers were arranging the crates of fish with what was already on the boat. Before he had brought the last crate onto the boat, the docking lines had been undone. The boat was finally underway with the extracted ones safely onboard.

The businessman had left western clothes and shoes for the family on his boat. They changed into those as the boat was going to Port Said. This was very necessary since part of the extraction plan was to have an American officer from the U.S. cargo ship meet them on the dock at Port Said with American passports for the family. The captain of the commercial boat phoned ahead to the U.S. cargo shop as it was preparing to dock. The officer from the American ship could now meet the docked boat with the passports inside the folder of commercial papers needed to load his ship.

Even though the passenger ramp to the U.S. cargo ship was momentarily blocked by the secret police wanting to examine the papers of the American seamen, the family was able to get their American passports from the ship's officer and board without incidence. The delay was very stressful as they waited for the secret police to look at their passports; however, they were finally allowed to board the U.S. cargo ship. The three family members, once onboard, began crying both for joy because they had successfully escaped and for relief because they would not have to endure more fear and uncertainty for their lives.

As the ship steamed toward Haifa, he explained to the extracted ones that they would have a cursory debriefing there by both American and Israeli intelligence personnel. He emphasized to them that they had to answer any questions fully and without hesitation. Most of this initial debriefing would consist of their telling what they knew about the regime from which they had escaped and not about their personal problems they had endured. The debriefing at the American embassy in London, however, would be a thorough and in-depth one conducted by several people from Langley.

He told the family that they had acted courageously and that what they would reveal in their debriefings would be of great use for planning by Langley. He thanked them for following well his instructions and for trusting him, a stranger, who had entered their lives. They never heard from him again though they often spoke of him and wondered where and how he was.

THE STREET LAMP

He had never questioned his assignments in his long career as a clandestine agent with the Central Intelligence Agency; however, this one seemed rather odd. There was, he knew, another good clandestine agent in a close-by country who was more than capable of doing this particular extraction. Since he was in a country far from the targeted country, he wondered why the insistence that he be assigned to this extraction was so paramount to Langley. He had heard that the agent, because of wounds suffered when he was younger, had slowed him down considerably as he became older, but would still accept high-risk assignments.

Only Langley could - and would - make a proper determination always using metrics which so many agents had railed against when it came their time to be told to retire as a clandestine field agent. Their bodies had also come to that conclusion, but their minds refused to accept the end of a challenging career. They knew that the mistakes made because of physical limitations would place too many people in untenable situations. Not only would it place the assignments in jeopardy but it could cause innocents to be placed in mortal danger. These factors Langley could never accept.

After his briefing on this assignment at the embassy in the

country where he currently was, he understood why the other clandestine agent could not have been chosen. It was a pity that the decision was based solely on his physical condition because mentally he would have been more than capable. The agent would have reluctantly agreed that he could not be given this assignment. Though they had never met and did not know one another, he could spend a few hours with the other agent; however, Langley prohibited this for very good reasons. There would be no secure place they could meet outside of headquarters. Arranging that would displace too many people and events for a purely personal reason. Also both knew that the movement of two clandestine agents to one place would likely attract the wrong kind of attention.

He had been told at his briefing that the person he was to extract was the only daughter of the vice premier of a small, but dangerous, far eastern country. She had been educated in the West, and was very fond of luxury clothing and perfumes which could not be gotten in her country. She was valued because she would be a window into the obscure and enigmatic ruling government. She had been previously contacted by another government friendly to the US. She finally agreed to defect but only with many concessions: a house with servants, car with a driver, and an enormous monthly stipend. Before final arrangements had been made, she made it known through the Swiss embassy that she would only defect to America. He was also told that everywhere she went — including the huge family compound in her country — she was accompanied by a heavily armed two-person security detail.

While attending a well-known European university, she lived in a luxurious apartment. Her security detail stayed in an apartment on the same floor. She went home twice a year on an airplane supplied by her government. After being at the university for two years, she was forced to return to her country and to remain there for three years. She was then given a position in her country's embassy in a former communist country in central Europe. She was to observe the use of capitalism in this country and how it affected both the government and its citizens. He learned also from his briefing that she enjoyed going to evening parties at the Swiss embassy where she mixed easily with foreigners. Langley, as usual, had prepared a thorough background on the targeted person.

He knew from his briefing that approaching her would be rather difficult. He hoped that he would be able to speak with her at the Swiss embassy's soirees. Since the targeted person mixed easily with foreigners, this would — at least in the beginning — be his first choice in becoming acquainted with her. This would also give him ample opportunities to observe others who might be attempting to speak with her. He was told that, after he had established a firm and comfortable relationship with the targeted person, he was to go to the American embassy where he would be given complete instructions on how to extract her without arousing undo suspicions from her embassy.

Langley had arranged for him to be given a German passport with a commercial attache' status. Since she was purposely sent to the country in order to observe both the use and effects of capitalism in a former communist country, he believed his being a commercial attache' with a western country's embassy would provide him a natural opening in speaking with her.

He was told in his briefing to fly from his current location to a neighboring country where he would take a train to a border town. There he would take a bus to the capital city of the country where the targeted person was. It would be a circuitous trip; however, it would afford him the necessary anonymity which he always needed. His German passport with a commercial attache' status would allow him entrance into both countries with little scrutiny from immigration officials.

When he arrived, he went to the German embassy where he presented his commercial attache' papers which, of course,

Langley had provided showing that he had served in several countries as a commercial attache'. He was then instructed to go to the cultural attache's office where he was told that there was only one hotel in the city which allowed foreigners to stay. This was a hold-over requirement from the former communist regime to keep track of all foreigners who entered the city.

He took a taxi to the hotel where he quickly noticed in the very large lobby that there were foreigners from many different countries - some of whom would be agents from intelligence groups of various countries. The hotel had a well-appointed dining room as well as a small cafe'. He was given a large room on the second floor which faced a fire station and a taxi stand. He, from long habit, went through his room looking for listening devices. He found three: one in the receiver of the old-fashioned black telephone, one under the bed, and one behind the door of the bathroom. All were well camouflaged and also high-tech. He removed them easily before he went down to the cafe'. He left one in the elevator in the control panel and placed one in the magazine rack where he bought a local newspaper. He placed the third one under a table in the cafe' where he bought a cup of coffee and a sweet roll. He thought those placements might confuse the ones who were listening.

As was his custom, he left the hotel and began walking in a quadrant of several blocks in order to observe people, places, and things in his new environment. In an intuitive manner he memorized everything he saw. This provided him with knowledge which no briefing, or for that matter maps, ever could. Often in his long career as a field clandestine agent tasked with extractions, these close-up observations had many times proved invaluable.

On his slow and purposeful walk, he noticed pot-holed streets with few working traffic signals. On the other hand, there were very few private cars on the streets. There were very noticeable government vehicles going beyond the non-enforced posted speed limit. He noticed that there were almost no electric tram cars, but there were busses belching black smoke from their ancient and tired diesel engines. Apparently the effect of capitalism which the targeted person was studying had not reached the streets and local public transportation. He also noticed that there were many blocks of drab apartment buildings with rows of bicycles near each building with no cars parked anywhere. Most of the street lamps were malfunctioning: some sporadically lighting up, some not working, and some on even during daylight.

He went into a few shops to observe both people and what was available in the large capital city. Shoppers were queuing for almost everything. There were few fresh items for sale and almost no meat. He noticed that there were no western imported goods - either food or dry goods. In another shop where he bought a shirt, he saw that there were almost no choices in clothing. Both the shoppers and clerks there were sullen. He could not blame them.

He learned from a man and woman standing outside the clothing shop that there was a bountiful farmers' market on the outskirts of the city. They were walking to a taxi stand and invited him to go with them. They spoke both English and German fluently. They explained to him that both had been in the former communist country's diplomatic corp. When the regime was overthrown, they were removed from their posts. They now lived on their meager government pensions in addition to doing sporadic translation work for extra and needed income. Both told him that the new government was slow in implementing the promised new policies of capitalism and freedom such as speech and press. The farmers' market they were going to was, however, an excellent example of everything the citizens longed for.

Their discussions with him were open and friendly. He knew they could be a good source of information for many things. As they got out of the taxi, he asked them if they would like to have dinner some evening. They responded by telling him they would if he first had dinner with them tonight. As they walked through the farmers' market filled with fragrances from smoked pork, fresh vegetables, and many varieties of fruit, he told them he would if they would allow him to purchase the food for the evening meal. When they agreed rather quickly, he realized that their income must be meager. He did not want to misuse this opportunity; so he asked them to choose what would be good for their dinner. He wanted to establish and maintain this friendship for the information about current events and people they would be able to give him.

He bought two kilograms of smoked pork butt, many tomatoes, a bag of onions, carrots, and several fruits. As they rode back toward the city center on an old and laboring bus, he noticed that everyone on the bus had purchased various items at the farmers' market. He wondered if the now three year old elected government noticed the vitality of something so simple. He also wondered if the targeted person ever came to this hub of capitalism.

After the delicious dinner in their small apartment, the woman came out with a carafe of home-made plum brandy. Several drinks later both of them began discussing their views of the current government. They were especially upset with all the foreign consultants the government had hired as well as the very obvious embassy employees from most of the countries in the capital who seemed to be asking questions of the citizens often and everywhere. They singled out with both scorn and admiration a very pretty woman who always had brusque security with her. They told him she was from a far eastern country where there were no freedoms. They told him that she had been several times to the farmers' market where she would interrogate the vendors about their views on what the free market meant to them.

They told him she reminded them far too explicitly of the elite of the former communist regime. She always appeared at the farmer's market in a Mercedes sedan with armed security. They did say, however, that she mingled well with both the vendors and shoppers as she questioned them about their experiences in the market. The most important information they gave him was that she was there early on Saturday mornings when the crowds were large. She was there usually from 7:00 a.m. until 9:00 a.m. They ended by telling him, laughing, that she was dressed as though she were going to a party at an embassy. This information gained from a chance encounter which he took advantage of would be very useful in his initial attempt to meet the targeted person.

When he returned to his hotel later that evening, he saw two large Mercedes sedans parked immediately in front of the door which effectively blocked all other vehicles from being close to the entrance. He recognized from experience that the occupants of the cars would be reasonably important and definitely have armed security. The reception desk was condoned off with four armed security personnel around the area. As he walked past the closed area, he saw that there were a man and woman being checked in by an assistant. From their language and clothing, he knew they were from the country of the targeted person. When he scanned the area, he saw her standing with two other officials from her country. She was elegantly dressed in western clothes. She was wearing a diamond bracelet on her left wrist and a Rolex watch on her right wrist. This meant she was left-handed; this was information which might be useful later for him.

She was very self-assured as she spoke with both the ones checking in and the two other officials. She ignored the security detail only because she was accustomed to having them around. She was taller and much prettier than the three photos he had been shown of her in his briefing. She would have quite easily passed for a southern European. He noticed that the two checking in and the two officials were almost deferential toward her. The hierarchy she belonged to in her communist country carried over to her present even though all were thousands of miles from their country. He thought that the engrained and forced control was totally pervasive.

As he watched the scene, he noticed that both other foreigners and the locals who were there were openly contemptuous of what was going on. Their country was now free of the previous dictatorship, and they very obviously did not want any reminders of enforced imperious privileges. Soon a local man and two women began singing — very off-key — the national anthem of the targeted person's country and inserting vulgar words into it. Even though the officials checking in along with their assistant and the two officials accompanying them heard the revised edition of their national anthem, they pretended they heard nothing. The targeted person simply smiled, and the security people scowled but did nothing to stop the impromptu rendition.

The targeted person briefly looked at him and did not smile or offer any acknowledgement that he was also looking at her. She had the look about her that she, being the only daughter of the vice premier, knew she could do many things which none of the others could even dream of doing. He wondered if her father knew she wanted to defect. The ripple effect of that would be a wholesale purge by the dictator of her country. In some way he admired her; however, he knew he had to be very cautious in approaching her so that she would not be harmed.

When the registration was complete, the security detail escorted all of them out to the waiting Mercedes sedans. She was the last one to leave the lobby. As she left, he noticed that she was somewhat reluctant to go with the entourage. She had tasted freedom and did not want to be under constant surveillance. He hoped that this would help him when he began the slow and cautious task of meeting her and explaining his presence.

His briefing did not include much about her personal life: whether she had any friends or what her real interests might be. He knew that he would need to learn these things about her. The large difficulty was that he would be severely limited in access to her when she might be alone. He decided that, with his German commercial attache' status, he would go to her embassy and attempt to speak to her embassy's commercial attache' about importing goods from Germany. This would give him the possibility of seeing her and allowing him to introduce himself. If the commercial attache' was interested, he knew that any negotiations on possible trade with the targeted person's country would, of necessity, take several weeks. This would give him ample opportunities to meet her and begin conversations.

The next morning he left his hotel and walked the two kilometers to her embassy. He presented his commercial attache' papers and requested to see his counterpart to discuss possible trade. As he waited, he noticed huge posters of the dictator on every wall. The embassy personnel would look on the large portraits with their faces looking as though they were in the presence of a god. All of the employees in the lobby were male. At every door leading from the lobby there were armed security. He was escorted to the door of the commercial attache's office where he was searched by the armed security man. He was finally let into the office where a female assistant asked him to sit until she spoke with the attache'. He noticed that there were three cameras on the walls of her small office with the obligatory portrait of the dictator. Her desk was neatly organized with various folders and no telephone. He saw no ballpoint pens, and the typewriter was a manual one. He thought he would give her a nice ballpoint pen when he left.

She finally returned to where he was sitting and told him he would have about twenty minutes to present his business proposal to the attache'. His office was larger but sparsely furnished with no decorations with the exception of a very large portrait of the dictator. It was on a wall where both the attache' and any visitor could easily see it. There were two telephones on his large desk as well as a tray holding four cups, a creamer, and a sugar bowl — meant no doubt for tea. On a table to the attache's right was an electric pot for heating water. Near that was a glass container filled with loose tea leaves. Interestingly, on the left side of his desk near a window was a small table with one drawer and nothing on it. He committed these seemingly innocuous things to memory.

The commercial attache' was short, wore glasses, and had an ill-fitting western suit on. He limped noticeably because his left leg was shorter than his right one. As he offered the agent tea, he attempted to make small talk about the weather and the general lack of various foods he was accustomed to. He asked the attache' about his family and how long he had been posted in this embassy. The attache' smiled for the first time when he spoke of his family. He had two adult children and three grandchildren all of whom were living in his country. He asked the agent if he was married and frowned when he was told he was not married. The attache' told him he had studied business as a graduate student at Moscow State University. He asked him if he had enjoyed his time there, and the attache' answered firmly that he had not. The language, people, and food he could not stand. He thought the Russian professors were prejudiced against his race. Also he had been in a severe car accident which broke his left femur in three places.

He asked the attache' if his country needed anything which could be imported from Germany. He asked the blanket question in order to give the attache' room to maneuver with his answer. The attache' smiled weakly while explaining that his country was working toward self-sufficiency; however, because of some international sanctions there were items which the great leader might approve. He further explained that any imported goods would have to be sold with favorable credit terms. He finally mentioned carefully because the meeting was being filmed with audio — that his proud country might need items such as wheat, automobile tires, and refined petroleum products. The agent told him he would return in a few days with proposals from German suppliers. The attache' was visibly relieved to hear that. He suggested that the agent return in four days. He explained that this would give him sufficient time to discuss the possibility of these imported items with the correct officials in his country.

As he left the attache's office, he was told that all trade proposals coming from his office had to be approved by the vice premier's daughter. When the agent heard this, he realized that many of the problems concerning meeting her had just been solved.

He would go to the German embassy and would get several trade proposal sheets. He would fill them out and give the targeted person the ones her commercial attache' had suggested as possibilities. He knew that any agreements would take six weeks or more; so he had no qualms about giving her what would amount to bogus proposals since he believed he would have extracted her long before then. He would make attempts at seeing her several times in her office and gradually gain her confidence enough that they could meet somewhere — perhaps at the farmers' market — and be able to converse out of earshot of her security detail. He wanted her to feel confident in him as a German commercial attache' and eventually as someone who could assist her in defecting safely. It would be a difficult balancing act for him.

As he left the attache's office, he noticed that there was unusual activity in the reception room. Six armed security men surrounded an obviously frightened man who had his arms up in the air as he was pleading to any who would listen that a mistake had been made. He shouted that he had been coerced into going to the American embassy. He attempted to explain that he had been told by his superior here at his embassy to go there in order to ascertain the number of Marines stationed inside the American embassy. He also said he was to take surreptitious photos inside with a micro camera he had been given. What his superior and he did not know was that as soon as he passed through the electronic doors of the American embassy, his hidden camera was signatured by the high level intensity of the magnetometers. He was stopped and searched. After his camera was removed from his clothing, he was questioned briefly; photographed; and escorted out of the building.

His shouted pleas fell on deaf ears. The commercial attache', who had followed the agent out to the melee, told him with an understatement that the embassy now had a problem. If the man were sent back to his home country, he would be summarily executed but not before revealing the name of the one who had ordered him to go on the small mission. The larger problem was that no one knew if his superior wanted to defect. He would be tortured in the embassy to ascertain his intentions. Only then would a very mortal decision be made concerning the underling now in custody.

The commercial attache', who was standing next to the agent, told him in a low voice that the temptations of the West with all of its freedoms were too much for many of his compatriots. All of them lived and worked in fear basically of each other. The urge to leave was never well-balanced with the desire to please the home country's dictator. The attache' ended his short and furtive conversation by saying that all were suspects in their daily lives. By then the man in custody was dragged roughly out of the reception area all the while shouting that he was innocent. No doubt he was the agent thought.

As the area was quickly cleared of both surprised visitors and anxious workers, he saw that the vice premier's daughter was looking intently at him. He knew she would have been told that he was a German commercial attache' here to present a business proposal. He also knew she realized acutely that he would likely report the disturbance and its probable sequences to the German embassy. He wondered how this would affect her desire to defect. He believed these events should make it somewhat easier to approach her. It would all depend on her ability to forego the knowledge of being executed if she were suspected of wanting to defect much less if she were caught.

He was not overly surprised when he saw her walking toward him. He guessed that she would apologize for the scene he had just witnessed. She motioned for her two armed security men to stay back as she walked toward him. He noticed her very western clothes and smelled the fragrance of Chanel Number 5 on her. These were not items which her commercial atache' would want to import. She had an unmistakeable aura of superiority which coupled with her attire and fragrance gave the immediate impression that she was a person of importance.

As she firmly shook his hand, she welcomed him to her embassy and hoped he had a good meeting with the commercial attache'. She finally mentioned the chaotic scene he had seen by saying that it was unusual and that everything which caused it would be properly taken care of. She did not say how. He told her he would appreciate it very much if he could meet her both in her embassy office and outside of the formality of the embassy to discuss what he had proposed to the commercial attache'. He wanted her to understand that he recognized that she was in a position to approve what might be allowed as imports into her country without actually saying it.

She agreed to meet with him for trade discussions; however, she told him she preferred meeting with him somewhere where there would be little notice of their being together. She then suggested meeting at a cafe' about two kilometers from her embassy. She explained that it was a very popular place for the international community to patronize. Besides, she added, the French croissants are quite delicious. He asked her if the day after tomorrow in the evening around 8:00 p.m. would be convenient for her. She readily agreed; again shook his hand with a firm grip; and said she was looking forward to their meeting.

He knew then that she wanted to be with someone from the West — and not necessarily to discuss trade. Even though she had basically initiated wanting to meet, he understood that he would have to move in increments with her to gain her trust. Not the least would eventually be the revealing to her that he was not a German commercial attache' but was connected to the American embassy. He would, he decided, continue to suggest — casually — meetings with her both at the international cafe' and the evening parties on the weekend at the Swiss embassy. By slowly gaining her trust, he would be able to gauge her commitment to defecting to the United States. She was, no doubt, constantly monitored even though she was the vice premier's daughter. This would have to be carefully worked around. She shook his hand for a third time, and told him she would be at the international cafe' the day after tomorrow at 8:00 p.m. He told her it was a good time and that he was looking forward to the French croissants. She smiled at that comment and walked away.

When he returned to his hotel, he sat drinking a cup of coffee and reading the local newspaper as he observed both arriving and departing guests. He wanted as much as possible to know who was in the hotel. He did not see any western guests — only those who were from the far East and neighboring countries. Few of them appeared to be not associated with the embassies in the city, and none of them were tourists as far as he could tell. It was important for him to be aware as much as possible of those around him. Through years of experience, he made his observations unobtrusively.

He decided that he would not ask the targeted person any questions at the international cafe' with might place doubts or concerns in her mind about him. Even though it had been she who suggested the meeting — and this was a sound reason why he knew she was still interested in defecting — he did not want to broach that subject until several meetings with her had occurred. It was exceedingly important that she fully trusted him. He would not have a second chance with her.

He knew also that he would have to meet with her at least twice in her embassy to avoid any suspicions from those who were monitoring her movements. There was no doubt whatsoever that her two armed security detail reported to the head of security in her embassy where she went and with whom she spoke and for how long. He needed to make their meetings seem natural.

When he arrived at the international cafe' a few minutes before their agreed-upon time of 8:00 p.m., he found it to be very crowded. The ambient noise would make it much easier to speak with her without being overheard. He finally found a small table with two chairs located about ten feet from the raucous bar. As he waited for the targeted person, he scanned the cafe' for any people who looked as though they were not there for an evening of pleasure. He looked especially for those who were standing along the walls of the cafe'. He saw six men who were standing and looking over the crowd. He would, without being obvious, keep both their locations and any movements under surveillance. He knew they would have been from intelligence groups of various embassies. Nothing seldom changes in this business he thought.

The targeted person showed up just a few minutes after 8:00 p.m. with her two armed security detail. When they came, he noticed that the six men whom he had identified earlier at once looked toward her and her escorts. That proved his suspicion concerning who they were. Two of them left their position and moved toward the targeted person. On purpose each of them bumped into her detail in an effort to see if they were armed. This meant two things to him: they were from the same embassy and they knew of the targeted person. The two men correctly apologized for their bumps and moved slowly across the cafe' toward another wall. Her security detail frowned briefly and moved closer to her without appearing to be annoyed.

He stood up from the small table so she would see him. When she saw him, she waved and smiled broadly. It was quite obvious that she was well-known at the cafe'. Several people spoke briefly to her as she made her way toward him. She gestured toward a waiter who then followed her to his table. He heard her tell him to bring two croissants and two cappuccinos. She had wasted no time in ordering. The very busy waiter told her the items would be brought to the table at once. She exuded the confidence of one who was very much accustomed to being listened to and then obeyed.

She was dressed in a very western white pant suit with a pale blue blouse. Her ensemble contrasted beautifully with her dark hair. He stood up and remained standing as she approached the table — both to welcome her and to observe quickly the ones along the walls and her armed security detail. He guessed correctly that her security personnel would remain near their table. One looked constantly at their table, and the other stood with his back to the table watching the crowed cafe'. Neither spoke to her or him.

Her first words to him surprised him somewhat. She told him how glad she was that he was there and that she looked forward to their first nonofficial meeting. This was, to him, an indication that she was exploring all options available to her for an eventual defection. Though he surmised this, he knew he had to proceed with caution tempered by nonchalance in this initial conversation. He needed to gain her confidence so that she would not feel any overt pressure. He told her that he was also glad to be here and that he was looking forward to the French croissants she had so highly praised. When he said this, he could see her visibly relaxing. He complimented her on her clothing saying it was unique to what he had seen since he had arrived. She quickly and firmly told him it was an effort to order her clothing from Paris because of the imposed dress code at her embassy. She managed, she said, with the help of her father.

Toward the end of their conversation which lasted some ninety minutes, he asked her if they could meet in her embassy to discuss the trade proposal. She readily agreed to meet in two days. She said too many people would become very suspicious if they only met outside the embassy, and that would include these two as she gestured toward the security men. As she got up to leave, he asked her if she would be interested in meeting at the farmers' market at some point. He told her he could recommend the smoked pork as highly as she did the French croissants. For the first time she laughed and told him that this coming weekend would be fine with her. With that comment she stood up and shook his hand. He noticed that none of the six men along the walls followed her out. That relieved him because it meant that their visit was viewed as only social.

When he arrived at her embassy two days later, he once again was searched; however, he was quickly escorted into her office where she, instead of sitting behind her large and ornate desk with two telephones on it, was sitting in a cushioned chair near a window. She got up and gestured for him to sit in the other chair. There was a table between the two chairs with a tea set on it. She asked him if he would like some imported Earl Grey tea from England. He realized that this was another example of her wanting to distance herself from her own country. He did not ask her how she managed to get the tea knowing that the others in her embassy would have to make do with cheap black tea from their country. He thanked her and told her he would like very much a cup of Earl Grey tea.

She was animated during their initial conversation; but when he attempted to steer their talk toward his business proposal of what the embassy would approve to be imported from Germany, she seemed as though she had almost no interest in it. She finally told him to present his proposal to the commercial attache' and she would approve it. He did not press her because he realized she was focused on wanting to know more about life in the West. She stood up indicating their meeting was over. As she walked with him to the office door, she asked him if he had ever been to the war-mongering country of America. He knew at once that she had given him a heads-up that there were listening devices in her office and not to discuss anything beyond the proposed business.

At the door she said she wanted to give him her business card. He thanked her for it and left the embassy. When he had walked several blocks away and saw no one following him, he looked at her business card. On the back she had written — obviously before he got to her office — "Please do not forget to meet me this Saturday at 7:00 a.m. at the farmers' market." He knew then for certain that she wanted to discuss much more than the price of the smoked pork. He would let her guide the conversation; and if it were about her leaving, he would suggest they meet Monday evening in the noisy international cafe' where he would present to her the precise plan for her defection. During the day on Monday, he would go to the American embassy both to bring the necessary people up-to-date and receive exact instructions on removing the targeted person and also how he was to leave the country.

He arrived a few minutes before 7:00 a.m. at the farmers' market. She arrived with her ever-present security detail at exactly 7:00 a.m. He walked toward her car before she got out and was stopped by her security people. When she got out, she told them to follow her several meters behind. As they walked through the outdoor market, she told him that she had studied two years at the Sorbonne. He said he now knew where her love for French croissants came from. She laughed at that comment and said it was true.

He saw that she was grateful to be out of her embassy. She spoke with an openness which he did not expect from her. She commented frequently on the freedom the vendors had to sell their products at a price they had determined. She bought nothing; so he offered to buy her some local fruit as well as some of the fragrant smoked pork. She gladly accepted his offer and thanked him profusely.

He asked her if she had enjoyed studying abroad. She answered with a longing sigh that she had thoroughly enjoyed studying and being at the Sorbonne for two wonderful years. She told him without his having to ask her that she had studied economics and political science. She volunteered that she had been amazed at the joy and liveliness of the students — especially those from America. She admired their freedom to criticize both their leaders and government without fear. She told him she had never before encountered that. She had many freedom-filled discussions with the American students. She told him that the very idea of democracy intrigued her so much that she read Alexis de Tocqueville's <u>Democracy in America</u> twice.

He now knew without any doubt that he could approach her about being extracted. He suggested that they meet at the international cafe' in two days. He told her he would like very much to discuss democracy's many attributes with her. She quickly agreed on meeting him there.

The next day he went to the American embassy to meet with his counterpart who was stationed there. He told him about his lengthy conversation with the targeted person. He told the stationed agent that he firmly believed she was now completely amenable to being extracted.

They discussed for almost two hours the details of the extraction and how he was to leave the country. He was to tell her at their meeting at the international cafe' that she was to walk in three days' time as though she was once again going to the cafe'. At the fourth street lamp from her embassy there would be a grey Peugeot pickup. She was to get in it and would be taken safely to the American embassy. There arrangements would be made for her to fly unannounced to the United States. He was instructed to tell her that, between the third and fourth street lamps, her two armed security detail would be neutralized by his counterpart.

He knew that he had to witness the extraction because of strict protocol for his briefing of events which would come as soon as he had left the country. He was told that a car with no diplomatic plates would pick him up at his hotel. He would be driven toward the extraction site at the fourth street lamp matching the exact time the targeted person would get in the Peugeot pickup. He would then be driven to the airport where he would fly directly to London. There he would give his briefing in the American embassy.

When he met her in the international cafe', he explained concisely all the details concerning her extraction. She listened intently without asking any questions. She thanked him profusely for giving her the opportunity to leave her stress-filled situation and go to the country which she had often dreamed of. She told him she would follow his instructions exactly. She said she would walk toward the international cafe' in three days' time looking for the fourth street lamp from her embassy.

He was picked up at his hotel at precisely the agreed-on time in a car with no diplomatic plates. As the car approached the extraction site, he saw the targeted person walking toward the third street lamp. As soon as she passed it, a car came near her two armed security detail. They both were quickly neutralized and put in the car which proceeded past her. At the fourth street lamp, she got into the waiting Peugeot pickup with no hesitation.

Though she did not see him, the last sight he had of her was an exuberant smile on her face as she began her journey to freedom.

TOWER BY THE SEA

The train, having left Varna on the way to Sofia, stopped suddenly without warning and with an ear-splitting shriek of iron against iron near Gorna Oryahovitsa. Coffee was spilled; lunches were sent flying from tables; and anyone standing outside his compartment was flung down the corridor of the well-appointed passenger train. In the confusion from babies crying loudly, woman shouting with dismay that their dresses were wet with coffee, men cursing for a ruined lunch, and some in the corridor moaning from broken bones; none noticed the uniformed state troops boarding the train almost before it stopped.

The passenger train had nine carriages, and two soldiers stormed into each carriage: one in the front and the other in the rear so that nobody could leave. The soldiers were heavily armed and were members of the elite force answerable to the regime's ruler. They rushed 12 passengers off the train. None of the unfortunate chosen seemed to fit any description of anti-government people. There were a man and wife perhaps in the their late thirties; an old man who seemed at best to be totally confused; a well-dressed woman of approximately 40 years old; and a young boy who was obviously in his late teens among the 12 shoved off the train. All were forced to kneel in the weeds next to the tracks. An officer approached them with a drawn Luger and, facing them, began shooting each in their foreheads. He had to reload his pistol before resuming his gruesome and remorseless act. During the short moment of his reloading, the young boy began begging for his life. The officer just laughed and waited to execute him last in order to prolong the boy's anguish. The summarily executed ones were left where they toppled over.

The officer, followed by two soldiers, boarded the train and began questioning each passenger with a loud voice demanding to know why they had been in Varna and why they were now going to Sofia. He examined closely the internal papers of the citizens and the passports of the non-citizens. All of the citizens cowered noticeably as they were relentlessly questioned. Their luggage was searched thoroughly without regard to any kind to replacing the contents: they were strewn on the floor. Some of the citizens were so frightened that they could barely speak. This made the officer very angry which resulted in even more invasive measures such as roughly searching people's clothing. This included babies and small children. The parents, obviously distressed at this treatment, could do nothing but acquiesce to the rude and intrusive actions of the officer.

The foreigners were, however, questioned by a man in a suit who took pleasure in asking very personal questions of them. He was very methodical in his questioning. He wanted to know why they had chosen Varna in which to have a holiday. He wanted to know the names of the hotels where they had stayed; whom they had met; whether or not they had accepted any invitations for dinner from citizens; and why they were traveling by train instead of any other mode of cross-country transportation.

After several hours of intense interrogation, the soldiers, officer, and the man in the suit left the train. As the train resumed its journey to Sofia, there was little conversation among the passengers. Each feared that a government spy might be among them.

The agent had been on a much-needed 10 day holiday after a particularly difficult assignment which had taken him to three different countries all belligerent to the U.S. He had been forced to use informants who had not been fully vetted by Langley. His many years working as a clandestine agent provided him with the necessary experience to use those informants. The extraction was difficult because the one targeted had to move quickly from country to country in multi attempts to avoid being caught, arrested, tortured, and finally executed. The extracted one was a very high valued person for both the U.S. and NATO and because of that profile, Langley had given their best clandestine agent this assignment.

He went to Edinburgh for a few days to enjoy the tattoo festival which he had seen and heard years before. Walking up the Royal Mile from the Palace of Holyroodhouse to the castle on the hill brought back vivid memories of more pleasant times. He rented a car and drove the approximately 50 miles over to Glasgow where he met a retired friend. They eventually took a ferry to the Isle of Arran where each brought a crofted sweater. As a fitting gesture to this part of Scotland, they went over to the Mull of Kintyre where they enjoyed a hearty meal at a pub.

After saying farewell to his friend once back in Glasgow, he drove back to Edinburgh where he checked in at the American consulate. He had to inform the station chief that he was no longer on holiday. He also wanted to know if there were a new assignment for him. He was told to go to the American Embassy in London as soon as he could. He bought a train ticket and left at once. As he traveled to London, he had to admit to himself that he was looking forward to his next assignment.

He met the station chief in the London embassy that afternoon. He had known the station chief for several years and trusted both his judgement and briefings. These were very important for a clandestine agent. The station chief began the briefing in the safe room by telling the agent that he would be leaving the next day for Sofia. He would be traveling with a British passport. He would also be taking a British passport for the female he was to extract. They would be traveling out of Bulgaria as a married couple.

Langley's intelligence had over a year of careful on-site gathering firmly established that the regime had been training assassins using a highly lethal poison to kill high-level officials in several western European countries. Langley had, through its many abilities, photographs of the known two dozen assassins. Langley had also pinpointed the training site located on the outskirts of Varna. Through careful and also cautious work, an informant had been identified and successfully recruited. The agent was to meet this informant after having been in Varna for several days. While staying at a large hotel where Langley wanted him to remain for six days, he would traverse the sea-side city observing three classes of people: citizens, non-citizens, and secret police. Through these observations he would be able to establish both physically and mentally the general mood of the city famed for its beaches and destination as a holiday place for eastern Europeans. He would be able to identify many things which would ultimately assist him with this assignment.

He flew from London to Prague the next morning via British Air. He was told in his briefing, since he was traveling as a British citizen, to use the national airline and not to fly directly to Sofia. He changed flights in Prague to Balham Bulgarian Airlines and boarded a Tupolev TU-134 plane for the flight to Sofia — but only after everyone's luggage was searched on the tarmac. As he had expected, it was full of eastern Europeans going eventually to Varna with its beaches on their holiday. He heard Russian, Czechoslovakian, and German languages on the crowded flight. The airline hostesses were surly and not at all responsive to any requests from the passengers. Emigration was reasonable quick since the government knew the passengers would be spending money in local businesses once they were allowed into the country.

    He took a taxi from the airport to the main train station located in the central part of the city. He was not surprised to see busy streets with lots of shoppers entering what appeared to be well-stocked stores. Tall apartment buildings were the predominate choice for living accommodation for people. He was pleased to see that they were not the Stalinesque style of apartment buildings so common in Bucharest. He saw few single houses; those he did see were large 19th century villas now occupied by embassies. The sidewalks were free of trash and other debris. Traffic consisted generally of taxis, delivery vehicles, trams, and quite a few Ladas. Everything gave the general appearance of a bustling and well-run capital city in a Communist country.

    When he arrived at the huge main train station, he bought a small lunch and a Pilsner from a very busy kiosk selling everything from food to newspapers to bouquets of flowers. After enjoying his lunch at a stand-up table with four university students comparing the influence of Petofi and Leopardi on modern poetry, he bought his ticket to Varna. His carriage was full of citizens going to the Black Sea resort to visit relatives: a married couple who was looking forward to telling their parents that they were finally going to have a child; a silent but well-dressed woman going to see her dying sister; a grandfather who had fought in WWII; an exuberant young boy perhaps 18 who had a job working as a life guard on a beach near Varna and would be living with his aunt and uncle. There were parents with babies, and single men attempting to flirt with the few single woman in the carriage. He thought this scene could be anywhere in Europe.

    Upon arriving in Varna, he took a taxi to the large hotel where he had been told to stay. Langley had made a reservation for him to be there six days. This would give him time to familiarize himself thoroughly with the city and also to observe the nationalities of the foreigners. By far the majority of non-citizens were from eastern Europe. Also the hotel had both a large dining room and two cafes. He had always made certain in his long career as a clandestine agent to eat in local restaurants simply because he could both observe the diners and listen to candid conversations. He also never failed to buy and read local newspapers wherever he was. He found that the newspapers were like a small but vivid window into local affairs.

The informant he was to meet on his third day was an east German whom Langley had recruited several years ago. Hans had moved to Varna from Potsdam after having experienced the pleasant weather during a chilly trip with his wife. He had no difficulty in obtaining a job in a tourist bureau translating brochures into German for the hundreds of east Germans who came yearly to Varna for its beaches and warm weather. After his recruitment as an informant, he had served as a very reliable source for not only local but also for national information which provided Langley with valuable knowledge there on the coast of the Black Sea.

Hans, in order to facilitate meetings with agents, had over the years always eaten lunch at the smaller of the two cafes in the hotel. The waiters had become accustomed to this; so when he met with someone, they assumed it had something to do with the travel bureau. He always spoke flawless Bulgarian to the waiters and read Bulgarian newspapers and magazines. By all appearance he looked and acted like a native. He had never aroused suspicion from the regime.

He met Hans at lunch on his third day in Varna. He had spent the first two days traveling around the beach city by tram. He would often get off and walk slowly for several miles in order to obtain a more clear feeling of the general mood of the native populace. The hundreds of holiday makers seemed thoroughly welcomed by shop owners, and he never saw any interaction of them with the local police. No wonder the East Germans loved coming here he thought.

Hans was having lunch as expected when the agent approached his table and exchanged an identification question with the answer from Hans. This was the protocol established by Langley years earlier for Hans. This easily confirmed both for Hans and any agent that each person was authentic. After he had ordered his small lunch of soup and bread, he asked Hans about the training of assassins using extremely lethal poison to kill their targets. Hans explained that there was a training site on the southern outskirts of Varna. He said that the assassins were both male and female. Hans told him that one of the female assassins was definitely in the small town of Balchik which was directly on the Black Sea.

It was widely believed that she may have inadvertently been pricked while training to screw the needle-like end onto a vial of poison while inserting the needled and closed vial into a hollow tip of an umbrella. This unfortunate accident had happened before to other assassins while being trained; however, since the regime wanted to continue using umbrellas with the concealed poison tip to assassinate high-level targets, nothing was changed in the training. The poison was so lethal that, without entering her bloodstream, it would have momentarily paralyzed her while making her very ill for several days.

Hans said she had not been seen at the training site for several days but that she had been spotted in Balchik where, no doubt, she was recuperating from her paralysis. She was in her mid-twenties and would not have been chosen as an assassin had she not passed an extremely rigorous physical examination; so the prognosis for her full recovery was very high. He also told the agent that she had been seen several times at the same cafe having lunch alone. Hans, at the end of his discussion with the agent, said he was convinced from talks with his reliable sources that the female assassin had managed to take a vial of the poison with her and that she wanted to defect.

He had been told in his briefing in London for this extraction assignment that a female assassin trained to use poison in a unique manner wanted to defect. He was to confirm this with the informant in Varna. He was to locate her and begin the extraction. His informant in Varna would be able to give him up-to-date information which was not currently available. It was known, however, that she had left the assassin training group for unknown reasons. It was suspected — but not confirmed — that she was in the small town of Balchik which was approximately 25 kilometers from Varna on the Black Sea. Beach patrols by the military were known from land sat photos. Their movement were exactly timed in the event he had to meet her on the beach.

He would have to use his experience to determine the best place to meet her in order to discuss the process of the extraction. He had first to locate her in Balchik without arousing any suspicions from either the local authorities or the military. It was very important that, if at all possible, a vial of the poison be gotten out of the country. Langley needed to analyze it so that an antidote to its effects could be developed. According to the land sat photos of the beach, there was a tower by the sea — quite likely a lifeguard tower — which now appeared abandoned. He was given a British passport as well as a British passport for the targeted person which had a close-up photo of her sourced from the land sat photos. He was finally told that they would, if the extraction was successful, travel out of Bulgaria as a married couple. they would travel from Balchik to Varna by bus, from Varna to Sofia by train, and from Sofia to London by airplane.

He took a local bus on the morning of his sixth day in Varna to Balchik. It was filled, as he suspected, with tourists who wanted to leave Varna for a smaller town on the Black

Sea. While most of the passengers were east Germans, there were several from France and England. There were no citizens on the bus. The 25 kilometer or so trip went very quickly even through he highway to Balchik was crowded with traffic. The bus stopped at the only bus station in town. The passengers collected their luggage and either looked for taxis or began walking to where they would be staying. There were no police stopping anyone; even the regime recognized that foreign currency spent by thousands of tourists prevailed over any harassment.

Instead of waiting for a taxi, he began walking along the sidewalks filled with tourists. He wanted to observe the town, its shops, its citizens, and the tourists. The little town could have been a typical holiday resort in southern France. There was no military presence in the town itself — any military would likely be patrolling the beach on the lookout for drug use and also for the buying and selling of drugs. They would also be very diligent in looking for and capturing citizens attempting to flee the country in small boats hugging the coast until Turkey was reached. These freedom-seeking journeys were usually done at night. He knew from his briefing that armed military was very prevalent on the beach. Any meeting on the beach with the targeted person would best occur no later than mid-afternoon. He preferred arranging for the necessary long meeting with the female assassin away from crowded cafes, and the beach near the abandoned tower would serve very well.

After he found the small pension, which catered to tourists from western Europe, where Langley wanted him to stay, he walked around the neighborhood looking for cafes in the general area. He had to know this since the targeted person had been seen regularly having lunch alone at several different cafes near the pension. He located six cafes where she potentially could have lunch. He then stopped at one; had a late lunch; and returned to his room in the pension.

The next day he left the pension early enough so that he would have time to walk by all six of the cafes he had found. If the one to be extracted appeared at any of those cafes, he would not miss her. As he approached the third cafe on his walk, he saw a lone female having coffee at a small table. He watched her for a few minutes to make certain that she remained alone and that nobody approached her table. She seemed preoccupied but not nervous. She was wearing sunglasses and smoking a locally-made non-filtered cigarette which she held easily with her long fingers. He approached her table in her line of sight so that he would not startle her. He asked her in his rudimentary Bulgarian if he could sit with her. She answered in perfect English that, seeing all the other tables were taken, he could. He offered her one of his non-filtered Pall Mall cigarettes and left the pack on the table implying she could have it. She seemed pleased with his offer. He asked her if he could order a small lunch for both of them. She accepted and told him that nobody had ever done that for her. He knew then that she would not only listen to a discussion concerning her extraction but also trust him.

As they ate their lunch while making general and small talk; she told him that, if he were to walk on the beach, he needed to be aware of the armed police patrols there. She said her country had a sizable problem with its citizens leaving via the sea even though they knew the journey itself would be difficult after they had managed to elude the beach patrols and finally get on any kind of boat. She also began speaking longingly of going to live in London. She explained to him that her great uncle lived there. He had served as an ambassador in the foreign service of Simeon II, the former King of Bulgaria. Prior to the king being deposed, he had resigned and remained in London where he had met and married a British citizen. She had heard from him intermittently over the years. She told the agent it was her goal to leave Bulgaria and live in London.

This was the opening he needed to explain to her how he

would assist her in leaving. As he carefully presented to her what would be the necessary steps for a successful extraction, he noticed that she very visibly accepted what he was telling her. He asked that she meet him the next day in the afternoon on the beach near the deserted life guard tower. He finally asked her if she would be able to bring a vial of the poison with her. He was not overly surprised when she told him she had kept one vial when she was dismissed from the assassin training program. She said she had hoped then that there might be a way she could either leave her country with it or in some safe fashion get the vial out of Bulgaria. She thoroughly understood the dangers which she might face.

He began walking from his pension the next day in the afternoon to the beach. He found, as she and his informant had told him as well as the land sat photos he saw in his briefing, that there were armed patrols on the beach. As he walked along the crowded beach, he easily saw in the distance the tower by the sea. He hoped that the targeted person would be there by the time he arrived. Since there were so many people on the beach, it would not be difficult to meet and speak with her. When he was perhaps 30 meters from the designated meeting place, he saw her lying on a large towel very near the old life guard tower. He approached her and greeted her in English because he wanted to establish not only with her but anyone listening that they both were British citizens here on holiday. Since she spoke perfect English, that would be easily done.

He lay down next to her and noticed that she was smoking one of his non-filtered Pall Mall cigarettes. He began explaining to her the required steps for them to leave Bulgaria. They would leave the next morning taking the bus from Balchik to Varna. There they would take the train to Sofia. From Sofia, he told her, they would fly to London landing at Heathrow. He would accompany her to the American embassy where she would be debriefed. He finally gave her a British passport with her photo lifted from the close-up land sat photos. Her passport had the correct entry visa, and it showed her surname as his. They would travel out of Bulgaria as a married couple. He told her this would eliminate most problems they might incur. He told her that, as an ostensibly married couple, they would have to spend the night together in his pension. He told her to take only one small bag which could be carried on the bus, train, and airplane. He also told her not to wear clothing or shoes which might look too local. She accepted all of his explanations and directives without asking any questions. She said only that she was truly looking forward to leaving and being with her great uncle in London.

They took a taxi the next morning to the bus station. Only western European tourists seemed to take taxis; so this small effort provided them with an additional cover as a British married couple returning home. She had taken his advice and wore stylish clothing and shoes which would not be out of place anywhere in western Europe. Both the taxi driver and the one who sold them their bus tickets spoke to her in English. He hoped that the purchase of the train tickets in Varna would go as easily. He knew, however, that any potential problem could be in Sofia since buying airplane tickets — British citizens or not — to London indicated a finality to leaving the country.

The short 25 kilometer or so trip from Balchik to Varna went quickly and without incident. They spoke animately to one another about their holiday in the event any of the passengers on the bus were government informants. They took a taxi from the bus station to the train station in Varna. They found, as expected, that the train station was very crowded. Going by train to Sofia was the least expensive way to travel between the two cities; so citizens and visitors used the service frequently. After buying their tickets, they had time for coffee which they bought in one of the many cafes near the train station. Anyone seeing them having coffee would have thought they were foreigners. To make the subterfuge complete, she bought a picture post card near the entrance of the cafe.

They made their way along the train platform to their carriage. He had insisted that they book an open carriage so that he could observe the other passengers. This train trip to the capital was very important since it was the first large step out of the country for the extracted person. He wanted to use every precaution available. The carriage was full with 16 passengers sitting on each side of the aisle. Most of the passengers were a mixture of eastern and western Europeans. There were, he guessed 10 or so who were speaking Bulgarian. He identified those at once because, when the conductor came through their carriage checking both the tickets and passports of each passenger, he spoke Bulgarian to those. They were perhaps going to Sofia to visit relatives. He noticed nothing out of the ordinary in their carriage.
    As the train left the station, he saw that she visibly began to relax. She knew that they were on a through train and would not be stopping. While he also knew that, he did not relax; his many years of clandestine experience had taught him to remain constantly vigilant no matter any apparent calm circumstance. To do otherwise was to invite possible disaster.
    After approximately three hours and 150 kilometers of a non-eventful trip, they ordered a small lunch of cheese and croissants with a pilsner for each. The steward wished them bon appetite; smiled broadly at them whom he thought was a newly married British couple; and left humming some tune. The agent noticed that she spoke flawless English with the steward. He knew that she was not going to jeopardize her only opportunity at freedom. Not once during their lunch did she mention anything about leaving; she spoke only about being in England.
    He had been watching the mile markers so that he could estimate both how far the train had traveled and how far it was to Sofia. It was a well-ingrained habit which had served him well over the years whether traveling by car, bus, or train. It helped him keep a mental map of where he was. He knew

that the train was approaching Goma Oryahovista; and while it would not stop there; it would begin to slow down slightly.

The train, without prior warning, suddenly stopped. He understood through experience that the train would be boarded by armed militia. She had a frightened look as their lunch and beers went flying from their table. He told her to remain as calm as possible and to speak only English. He told her also to expect their passports and carry-on luggage to be thoroughly scrutinized by any who boarded the train. He was now hyper alert in the ensuring chaos as he watched where the heavily armed soldiers stationed themselves — front and rear of their carriage while four of them yanked roughly 12 of the passengers from their seats. All of those were Bulgarians: a couple, an old man, a woman, and a young boy among other scared-looking citizens. They were roughly forced off the train. They were then made to kneel down next to the tracks. A colonel with a drooping mustache approached the group and slowly removed his Luger from its holster. Facing them he executed all in cold blood. For some evil reason he executed the young boy last even as he was pleading for mercy. He laughed as he shot the boy in his forehead.

When the colonel entered the carriage after the executions, he was accompanied by a man in a suit who questioned each foreigner in the carriage minutely. He wanted to know where each had stayed in Balchik or Varna; he asked if any had had lunch or dinner in the homes of citizens; he inquired specifically why they were traveling by train instead of flying; and finally he examined each passenger's passport for any discrepancies concerning visas. The colonel, in the meantime, was removing everything from the passengers' luggage and throwing all the contents on the floor which had food, coffee, water and beer enmeshed into the carpet. He seemed to take pleasure in his actions since he knew that nobody could complain.

The man in the suit spent almost 30 minutes questioning

the agent and the female assassin closely — often repeating the same question. Their passports were in order with correct entry visas; so there was nothing there that would have caused any suspicion. He asked them where they lived in England; how they met; how long had they been married; where the usually went on holidays; and other personal questions which finally satisfied him.

The interrogation of the passengers took almost five hours. There was no escaping the intensity of the fear caused by the regime's personnel on the train. Even after they left, there was almost no talking among the frightened passengers for fear that one of them might be a planted government spy.

The agent knew that, because of the train's delay, they would miss their hoped-for flight. He told the extracted one that they would have to spend the night in a pension near Sofia's airport and take the earliest flight available the next morning to London. When the train finally arrived in Sofia, they took a taxi to the pension. She was exhausted from the trauma on the train and at once fell asleep fully clothed. He remained awake for several hours as he outlined mentally what was left to be done on the journey to London. The most difficult part would likely be any actions the government airport personnel would take. He had gotten her too close to freedom for all to end at the airport.

They took a taxi very early the next morning to the airport where he easily purchased their tickets to Heathrow. When it became time to board their flight, all passengers had to place their luggage on the tarmac and stand next to it. The luggage of each was searched before any could board. Nobody said a word as all waited for the 50 or so passengers' luggage to be searched. Only when that was completed were they allowed to board the airplane. There was a collective sigh of relief once all were onboard.

He and his female extracted assassin had no problems going through British emigration since they had British passports. When they were finally outside and waiting for a taxi to take them to the American embassy, she hugged him tightly and whispered that she had smuggled a vial of poison safely out. She explained that she had placed it between sanitary pads under her panties. He thought — momentarily — that he had known of most methods concerning smuggling items until he heard this ingenious method. He told her that she was brave doing that. He also told her that the debriefing officers at the embassy would be grateful for her courage. He finally told her Langley would now be able to analyze the poison and develop an antidote. This, he said, would rather quickly save many lives because of her intelligent action.

NIGHT OF WOLVES

There was a light rain falling on the mostly deserted streets as he walked from his hotel room to the embassy that early summer morning where he was to be briefed on his next assignment. It had taken him two days to arrive because he was told to fly from his previous location in the opposite direction from this city and then take a most circuitous route via trains to this new place. He understood that necessity because of his work, but it seemed a waste of valuable time.

He had carefully noted both at the departure and arrival airports whether anyone was following him. He watched especially closely each time he had to change trains if he recognized someone whom he had seen earlier. He had always been fascinated, that in this part of the world, by the very observable fact that those who would tail him made little attempt at being inconspicuous. He had developed over the years an acute ability both to note and evade those who would be following him.

As he walked to the embassy, he would occasionally stop at shops with large windows as though he were looking for something. This served two very good purposes: anyone following him would also stop or walk past him, and he could use the windows as reflections for activity across the street. While this was second nature with him, he was constantly amazed at the number of times those who were following him failed to observe his stopping to window shop.

He made certain that his way to the embassy was anything but straight. He crossed streets twice, and walked back in the direction from which he had just come. By doing this, he was able to notice if anyone was also crossing the street who had been on the other side. Everything so far seemed clear. With that qualified thought, he walked to the street just parallel to the plaza on which the embassy was located.

The foreign national guards on the outside of the embassy grounds waved him perfunctorily on seeing that he was not a citizen of the country. They were there to prevent nationals from storming the embassy. They would have orders to shoot their compatriots first and ask questions later. It was a good defense before the U.S. Marines had to become involved.

When he got to the entrance of the embassy, he informed the stern looking Marine in his dress blues that he had an appointment with the commercial attache'. He said nothing more to the dressed-in-blue Marine. As he entered the very large reception area, he noticed quickly the usual supplicants: harried travelers with lost passports, Americans who wanted to marry a native, and the natives who wanted desperately a visa to go to America. It would be the same in any American embassy he thought.

In spite of his purposeful meanderings from his hotel room to the embassy, he arrived within five minutes of his scheduled appearance. He stood to the far right of the long and curved appointment desk. It was important that he not be too early because he would have attracted unnecessary attention from those sitting and waiting. If he were late by only ten minutes, his appointment would have to be cancelled because of the intricacies of far-reaching time zones involved and of the ones who would have a very small window to connect on a quick telephone call.

Almost to the minute, an obviously armed man in a suit came up to him and asked him the name of his favorite NBA team. After answering the innocuous question correctly according to a prearrangement, he was told to follow the suited man. He was taken down a highly polished tiled corridor to a door which opened to two elevators and which were guarded by armed Marines. He and his questioner entered the elevator on the left. It went down three floors to a sub-basement area. After leaving the elevator, he was led to another guarded door of a floor to ceiling steel vestibule. After entering this small room, he had to pass through a magnetometer and also be quite thoroughly searched by hand.

The thick steel door to the meeting area was unlocked electronically. He was closely ushered into a room with crisscrossing baffles on all the walls and ceiling behind which was metallic layering which looked similar to small chain mail. The room was devoid of anything with the exception of an almost rectangular conference table with eight chairs on felt-covered wheels. On the table was a four-sided speaker which he knew was connected both to an encrypted telephone line and a recorder. The Marine and suited man who had ushered him in exited the silent room leaving him with the ambassador and station chief both of whom were seated at opposite ends of the table. He was gestured to sit in the middle with his back to the closed door. The lighting was such that there were no shadows. He quickly noticed prior to sitting down that there were what he surmised were cameras in small openings on the walls and ceiling as well as on the recorder which, no doubt, had been activated as soon as the door had been electronically opened.

Though he knew the ambassador by name only, he was well-acquainted with his background from a lengthy briefing earlier in the year. He was very thankful that the ambassador was not a political appointee. Those, he had learned, were never fully knowledgeable about his type of work. This one had joined the State Department after his military service, and had worked his way up over two decades to being named ambassador. More to his satisfaction, the ambassador had been in intelligence in the military for six years. Now in his early fifties, he was not only competent but also confident.

He knew the station chief only because of a far-reaching disagreement they had had three years earlier in another country. The station chief had made statements which were contrary to what was, in fact, not only settled protocol but also potentially injurious to field operatives. In a heated meeting with the ambassador in that embassy, he had pointed out precisely and in detail what was wrong with the station chief's many comments. He openly questioned the man's sense of duty and regard for those under him. When confronted with the reasoned statements in the meeting with the ambassador, the station chief became excessively angry and threatened to derail the career of any who questioned him.

At this point the ambassador, who was a large donor to the President's election and had been the CEO of a large company in the states, told the station chief bluntly to shut up. The ambassador called the proper person at Langley, and told him the gist of the meeting's shouted comments. Langley told him to forward the recording of the meeting. The result was both predictable and swift: the station chief was sent to a country in which nobody wanted to work. He also had a letter signed by the Director outlining the action taken along with the reason for it being placed in his personnel file.

Later the same day, the reprimanded station chief told him that he would regret having made the comments and causing them to be reported to Langley.

He knew the ambassador at the meeting in the acoustically safe room would have been aware of his station chief's previous reprimand. He also knew that the station chief would be on his very best behavior. As he entered the conference room, he noticed that the station chief barely concealed a look of surprise at seeing him. He had not been told by the ambassador who would be doing the proposed extraction.

As he sat down, he saw immediately that the station chief avoided looking directly at him; instead, he feigned an aura of command while fidgeting with his name tag hanging on its lanyard around his thick neck. If the ambassador noticed anything odd in the station chief's demeanor and actions, he indicated nothing. Though he knew, and had read the report, of the station chief's vocal disagreement with the operative sitting at the table, he also knew the past must not be a part of what had to be done now.

The ambassador, without any preamble, began the meeting by outlining what he had to do before a final decision could be made. He told the two that he would call the Director at Langley who was six hours west of their location to get approval at the highest level for the assignment to proceed. He would then call the sole contact who was seven hours east of their location to tell him what the decision had been. He explained in a terse tone also what the operative already knew from his many previous assignments: that there would be an absolute denial of both his existence and any knowledge of anything which might implicate Langley. The ambassador knew from his detailed briefing that the operative would agree to those harsh terms. He would ask him first before telling the station chief to brief the operative on the proposed routes and contacts on the routes.

Neither the operative nor the station chief knew what the assignment would be until the phone call with Langley was concluded. The need to know extended to everyone simply because there could not be any failure from disclosures. The ambassador, a career State Department person with his prior military intelligence background, knew what the assignment would be. It would be left entirely for the station chief —- over a period of several days —- to develop the details of the assignment.

As the ambassador hand-dialed the very private number of the Director, he glanced at both the operative and station chief to see if there were any reactions to the procedure. The operative had no expression; however, the station chief looked somewhat surprised when the ambassador dialed the number instead of requesting someone upstairs to dial it. He had never before been involved in an assignment of this magnitude; so he could not have known -- or even guessed -- that the ambassador was required to dial the number. It was another level of security. His dialing was recorded by four cameras: one above him, one behind him, and one on either side of him. These images were already at Langley before the call was answered.

At the first ring from the Director's private and encrypted number, recordings began both in his office and in the conference room in the embassy. The recordings would continue until the call ended. The Director spoke first by saying the assignment had the President's approval and that he concurred with no adjustments. The ambassador acknowledged those decisions. He added that he would send the Director a description of the procedures the station chief and operative would develop. The recordings of the short conversation and the President's approval with the Director's concurrence would be delivered at 4 a.m. to the White House as part of the President's Daily Brief from Langley. All would, additionally, be kept in an eyes-only location at Langley.

The ambassador then hand-dialed the only contact the operative would have. There was an immediate answer of one syllable in an interrogative tone: go? The ambassador answered likewise by saying one syllable in a declarative tone: go.

The minute details for the extraction of the high-valued person had been developed over ten months. What had not been put together was how the operative would travel seven time zones east from the embassy. The station chief and he would develop all the details within three days prior to his leaving. They would outline a route with modes of transportation, safe houses, contacts, and methods of communication. All had to be redundant in the likely event that not everything would go as planned considering the distance and human errors by those involved in the intricate plans.

The one to be extracted was a person of very high interest to the United States. He was a nuclear physicist in his early sixties who was not in the best of health. His wife and only son had been executed by the authorities. He had been forced to watch both their torture and executions. The sole contact there had informed the chain of contacts that the scientist had rapidly deteriorated physically since the executions. The authorities had moved him inside the closed city to an old and small apartment where he was guarded day and night with only a physician allowed to see him once a week. He was transported daily in a military vehicle to his lab.

When Langley was informed of the developments, the ambassador was notified. That embassy was chosen because of its central location, and also because of the military intelligence background of the ambassador. Other embassies were not chosen because they were too close to the sphere of influence of the targeted country of the scientist. The operative was chosen because he was fluent in the language of the high-valued person, and also because he had the physical and mental abilities to carry out the very demanding operation. Everyone involved had to be accurate, knowledgeable, and trustworthy. All had to understand well what would happen if only one part failed.

The ambassador closed the meeting by telling the station chief and the operative that they had less than three days to put together a detailed plan for the extraction. When it was completed, Langley would have to approve it. After the approval, the operative would leave immediately. He emphasized to the station chief that the operative would have the final say on their plan. He also told them that they would develop the plan in the safe room, and that everything they said would be recorded and sent to Langley.

When the ambassador left the safe room, the station chief looked at the operative with a small smirk on his face. He knew that the operative would be completely aware of all nuances with everything they would discuss. He also knew that the operative was categorically trusted by both the ambassador and Langley. He further knew that the operative would remember their run-in of three years earlier. He wanted to gain the operative's confidence by appealing to his sense of dedication by pretending he had forgotten the past episode which had derailed his career. He would agree with everything the operative would suggest.

He, the operative, and the station chief began the plan by discussing first the distance: approximately 4,000 kilometers one way. He would have to travel by several modes of transportation while changing both directions and means in order to travel without being followed. They devised a plan which would allow him time to remain in several towns in order to make certain no one was aware of him. He would first fly to a neighboring country's capital and next take a train covering approximately 500 kilometers with two planned overnight stops. At the end of his train trip, he would take a bus into the next country in order to avoid lengthy travel by train where it would have been very difficult to disembark should he become suspicious of being followed.

When the bus arrived at the next border, he would face his first challenge: he would have to obtain an entry visa to the targeted country with specific reasons for entering. He suggested, with the approval of Langley, that he would state that he was on a business trip to sell much-needed imported items. Langley supplied him with a legitimate firm which was on a sanctioned list for trading. From there he would take a train to the first large town near his final destination. After spending two nights at a pre-chosen hotel, he would travel again by train to the outskirts of the closed city. There he would present his business credentials and business entry visa in order to obtain a special visitor's visa.

He would leave with five passports, one for each country, which Langley provided. Each passport had a photograph of him different from the previous one. He would leave with a full beard, and would shave at overnight stops to match the next passport's photograph. He would arrive in the targeted country clean shaven. After the use of each passport, he would destroy it. The only one he would not destroy would be the fifth one which he would use on his return with the person he was to bring out. This passport was from a country which traded with the targeted country. It also had stamped in it visas from several countries in addition to the needed exit visa. He would leave with money in coins and small bills from the four countries. He would take a small leather overnight bag lined with a very thin layer of lead. He would take no weapon.

The input of the station chief was limited to giving him the names and telephone numbers of ten contacts – two in each of the five countries. Each contact was given a password. The operative committed these to memory. Redundancy was built in the event one of the contacts had been compromised. Each of the ten contacts had been given a window of two days – 48 precious hours – when the operative would contact them. There was almost no room for delays. The operative, as always, was on his own with blanket denial should anything go wrong.

The plan was fully developed within the three days Langley had given them. Every detail was gone over several times. The distance traveled on each section of the trip was carefully calculated to coincide with the contacts' two day window. With his previous experience, the operative knew this could be the weakest part of the plan. No one could foretell if a bus broke down or if a train was somehow delayed. The two day window provided a redeeming chance to get back on schedule if needed.

The overriding factor for the success of the trip was that it would be done in the summer when the weather would not play an important role. Doing it later in the year would present difficulties which would be very hard to overcome.

He left the embassy at 6:00 p.m. and walked to the nearest tram station. He took the tram to a bus terminal where he took a crowded bus to the airport. He and his bag were hand-searched at security because he was a foreigner. His leather overnight bag was emptied but nothing was found to arouse suspicions. The other four passports were at the bottom under the thin lead lining in a very well-concealed compartment. The flight was uneventful. He took a taxi to the train station where he made his first contact using a pay telephone at 9:00 p.m.

He had decided he would travel about 300 kilometers of the 500 before he had his first overnight. He bought a second class ticket because it would put him in a crowded carriage with far fewer chances of being spotted. The train, which left the station at 10:00 p.m., was a local train which meant it would be making several stops at small towns. He soon joined a raucous group of travelers several of whom had packed dinners of various smoked meats, cheeses, and fruits. Copious amounts of home-made plum brandy were shared among the carriage passengers. Nobody asked him where he had been or where he was going.

The slow local train pulled into the station of the town where he would have his first overnight at 5:30 a.m. As he got off, he looked quickly but efficiently at the ones who were on the platform to welcome the arrivals. He saw no one who looked out of the ordinary. By the time he had left the station and begun walking along the already. awakened streets, it was a little before 6:00 a.m. He stopped at a small cafe to buy an espresso and local newspaper. While he was sitting alone at a table outside, he read the small paper and slowly drank his coffee all the while watching both who entered the café and those who were walking by. When he was finished, he went to a nearby telephone booth and called his next contact.

He then walked circuitously to the small hotel where he would be spending two nights. He registered easily because of the prearrangement Langley had made. He visually scanned his room for any tracking devices and found none. He shaved leaving a goatee and mustache to match the photograph on the next passport.

He awoke early and went walking to another café where he had a small breakfast after buying the local paper. He saw no one who had been on the overnight train; nor did he see anyone who lingered suspiciously at any table. He was satisfied that this part of the long and complicated trip was clean. He walked slowly back to his small hotel using a different route than the one he had taken to the café. He called his next contact from an isolated telephone booth.

The next part of his trip by train once again used a local train. It left the station at 8:00 a.m., and was scheduled to arrive at his next stop around 2:00 p.m. He was thankful that it would be early when he arrived because he would need daylight hours to walk to the bus station after registering at his hotel. He had to purchase his ticket to the border of the next country. He also wanted to scout two different routes to the bus station. All of this would take valuable time.

He walked to the train station without anyone following him. He bought again a second class ticket which would take him to the border town where he would have to obtain an entry visa into the targeted country. The carriage was packed with locals going to the large border town to sell and buy goods. He finally found an empty seat where he sat for the six hour journey. Nobody paid any attention to him.

The train arrived at the border town at 2:15 p.m. Everyone rushed off; so he had time once again to scan the people on the platform. He saw no one who looked out of place. Since he was going into the targeted country, he had to go to the immigration office in order to obtain his business visa. There were two officials in the office: a woman who asked him the usual questions about his travel plans; and an armed man who asked him about his company and the kind of imports he would be selling. The officer took at least ten minutes examining both his passport and his business papers. Just as the man was about to stamp the business visa in his passport, he asked how his company was invited to the closed city to sell imports. He answered by saying our common republics had to assist one another because the West would not. This satisfied the official, and he stamped the business visa in the much-scrutinized passport.

He left the immigration office and walked to a tram station where he got on a tram and rode it to within a kilometer of the pension where he would be staying one night. He got off at a small plaza where he was able to call his next contact. He walked the rest of the way to the pension. After eating a solid meal downstairs, he went to his room and shaved off the goatee leaving only the mustache. He then went for a walk along the streets which he would use in the morning to get to the train station. He preferred walking rather taking a tram so that he not only could observe people but also memorize landmarks for his walk to the train station early the next morning.

The train he would be taking to the first large town near his destination would leave at 5:00 a.m. with one long stop of approximately two hours about halfway there. Counting the stop, the trip would take a little over 11 hours. It was the only train scheduled to this town. Since the town was only 125 kilometers from the outskirts of the closed city, he knew that all passengers would be searched prior to boarding; and that at the two hour stop, all passengers would be required to leave the train while all the carriages were thoroughly searched. Before boarding for the last part of the trip, the passengers would not only be counted but also closely hand-searched by officials who had total power to detain any whom they had any suspicions about.

He got up the next morning at 4:00 a.m. and walked slowly along the well-lighted streets to the train station's ticket office. As always he did not take a direct path. The ones who were out this time of day were merchants going to the large market to purchase what they hoped they could sell that day. As he got closer to the ticket office, there were various vehicles from which travelers emerged. The line at the ticket office was already long. Each passenger had his internal papers examined before paying for a ticket. When it was his turn at the ticket office, the official at once noticed he was traveling with a passport rather than internal papers. He explained that he had permission to go into the closed city as a businessman. This satisfied the ticket agent, and he was given his ticket.

Before he boarded the train, he was searched and questioned about his stay in the large town at the end of the trip. He told the official he would be spending two nights in the town. He also gave the official the name of the hotel which the official then wrote down on a page with his name and passport number. He was told which carriage and compartment he would travel in. As he walked through the carriage to his assigned compartment, he noticed that at each end there was an armed guard. He knew it would be the same for every carriage. This prevented passengers from leaving their carriage to go to another one.

The other three passengers in his compartment were a husband and wife with their young son. They told him they were making their yearly trip to the son's grandparents. They further explained that it was a difficult journey for them because of the heavy security. They complained about that in low voices. He knew from their demeanor and conversation that they would present no problem for him. He told them briefly that he was going to the large town only to see a friend who was ill. They asked him no questions. Since it was early in the morning, they offered him a cup of hot and strong tea. He gave them a loaf of freshly baked bread which he had bought at a kiosk in the station.

After traveling about five hours, the train slowed down and stopped. An announcement was made telling everyone to remain in their compartments and wait. He looked out the window and saw an area about 30 meters wide which had no vegetation of any kind. There were tall poles set in the ground about the length of each carriage. Hanging between the poles was a metal chain to which was attached a leash leading down to a snarling dog who ran back and forth between the poles. The dog was accompanied by a heavily armed man who never ceased looking at the windows where the startled passengers were staring at the strange scene.

All the passengers with their luggage were escorted by armed guards off the train one carriage at a time. They were taken to a cavernous room where they were told to place their opened luggage in front of them and wait to be searched. They were also told not to speak to one another. The searches were very thorough and brusque. They took just under two hours. The passengers with their luggage were escorted by armed guards back onto the train one carriage at a time.

He now calculated that with this long stop and the scheduled stop of two hours at the half way point, the trip would put him arriving quite likely a little over 13 hours rather than 11 hours. It would be dark on his arrival. He knew the pension where he would be staying for two nights was about three kilometers from the station. This was chosen so that he could walk some distance to see if he was being followed. The only concern he had was that his next contact might not still be available because of the delay.

When the train reached the station in the small town for its two hour scheduled stop, he got off so that he could walk some and also find a café for what would be his only meal during the long day. As he walked away from the station, he noticed a man in a railroad uniform with a gray cap watching him. He paused for a moment to see if the man would leave. He did not. The problem now would be to lose him as he walked to the pension. As he crossed the street in front of the train station, he noticed another man who had positioned himself so that he could signal the man in the railroad uniform. He knew now that he was being followed.

At the first intersection, he crossed over to the other side where there were shops still open. He pretended he was looking at things in the window of one of the shops. He was, instead, using the reflection of the window to view back across to the sidewalk he had just been on. For a moment he thought there were only ordinary people walking home. In a few minutes, however, he spotted a man who was looking directly at him. That would be, he realized, the third one who was attempting to follow him. He went into the shop long enough that the third man began crossing the street. He then left the shop and crossed back over to the side where the man had been. He saw that the man did not notice his crossing the street; instead, the man went to the shop and then left.

He noticed that the man was using a two-way radio. This meant the ones following him were from the government. He did not understand how they knew of his arrival; and for that matter, how he had been compromised. All he knew at the moment was that he had to evade the four men successfully; find a telephone booth to call his contact; and to get, unseen, to the pension.

He went back the way he had gone using several different streets with reversals. When he was within 100 meters of the train station, he walked four intersections in the opposite direction he had first taken. When he was finally satisfied no one was following him, he turned down a street in the direction of the pension. He had to find a telephone booth to call his contact. There were usually booths at intersections; so he continued walking while observing others on the street.

When he was less than one half kilometer from the pension, he saw a telephone booth at the next intersection. He crossed the street and walked back half a block. Shops were beginning to close; so he had to pretend he was looking for a shop where he might buy something. Once again, he used the windows to observe people on the other side of the street. When he saw no one who looked as though that person was lingering without purpose, he walked down the sidewalk on the street he had just crossed.

As he approached the intersection where the telephone booth was, he noticed a man who entered the booth for a moment without making a call. The man then walked perhaps ten meters away and stood near a closed shop. He knew he had to go past the booth while closely observing the man. He walked quickly as though he was going home after a long day of work. The man turned as he walked past him on the other side of the street. When he got to the intersection, he crossed the street and walked toward the one who was watching him from a doorway of a shop. The man then walked away toward the intersection so that he could have a better view of the telephone booth.

He decided to walk past the telephone booth and double back. If the man was actually watching him, he would also have to move toward the booth. He noticed that the man kept walking away from the booth. He did not appear to have a two-way radio on him.

He knew he had to call his contact; so he walked toward the booth all the while keeping track of the man. When he saw that the man had continued walking away from the booth, he went quickly to the booth.

He used two of the local coins which he had earlier gotten at the embassy. He called his contact and gave his password. The contact responded with an incorrect one. He immediately hung up knowing something was wrong.

As soon as he hung up, the street lamp went out leaving the area around the telephone booth in darkness. He realized his assignment had been compromised. He heard footsteps running toward the booth. When he exited, he saw the four men whom he had earlier noticed rapidly running toward him. Each was armed with a long wooden baton.

The first one to reach him hit him across his upper back. He at once kicked the man hard and high up between his legs which caused him to bend over in agony and to drop his baton. He picked it up and hit the man under his chin breaking his jaw bones. He fell unconscious.

The second and third men attacked him viscously with their batons. He hit one full in the face causing the man to fall at once. He then used his baton to hit the other man across his neck crushing his trachea. Both did not get back up.

The fourth man, who had on the railroad uniform whom he had noticed at the station in the small town, lunged at him swinging his baton like a scythe. The man was so enraged that he did not see his intended target kneel down in the darkness. He hit the man on his left knee, and then hit him hard on the side of his head. He collapsed immediately.

When he was satisfied that the four men were unconscious, he wiped clean the handle of the baton he had used and dropped it among the four bodies. He then walked slowly away knowing he had been betrayed.

THE WATERING WELL

While Langley's most experienced clandestine agent had had previous assignments in all of the north African countries, one in particular had presented unique problems for the U.S. — not the least being the mercurial leader who, as a young colonel at the age of 27, had in a bloodless coup overthrown the king of a very poor country. He promised sweeping changes in most things which mattered to the populace: housing, education, and medical facilities. He had, in the beginning of his rule, soon removed all foreign troops from the country. He also closed some embassies and many consulates of those countries which he believed did not support both his rule and vision. He was in actions and appearance a very charismatic leader of a country generally recognized as backward in many respects. As the years passed, however, he quelled ruthlessly domestic dissent with imprisonments, tortures, and executions. He began to sponsor what he termed armed conflicts for freedom in various countries.

As he became emboldened by the lack of internal opposition and international pressure, he began openly inviting a large terrorist organization to establish a training camp in the country — which quickly grew to five large ones. He also proposed a union with a large neighboring country so that their combined militaries would be a deterrent to outside forces which he believed were almost omnipresent. He asked for, and received, from the U.S.S.R. not only tanks, large howitzers, and war planes but also strategically placed SAM sites along the coast of the country. As a final insult to the international community, he managed to have a NATO country train his pilots in the operation of Soviet MIG jets. He was, it seemed, impervious to normal conventions.

It was into this roiling maelstrom of outrageous behavior that Langley would send its best clandestine agent to perform an extraction which would turn out to be the most physically difficult one of his career. Since he had just completed an extraction and his subsequent debriefing at an American embassy in Europe, he was given a few days off before he had to go to Langley for the briefing on this new assignment. He spent those infrequent free days at a cabin of a friend on Lake Balaton. He then flew to Washington, D.C. via London.

His briefing at Langley was much longer than usual. He met with the Director who went into detail about this particular extraction. There were many overlying factors which had to be considered. Many had to be accomplished prior to the beginning of the extraction. He was shown Land Sat photos of the PLO camps and told his first objective in country was to infiltrate the largest of the camps and terminate the commander. He was told, as usual, that should he fail, Langley would deny his existence. He was given explicit directions to the camp and also how to approach it unarmed.

His greatest objective, however, was to locate and extract an educated Bedouin who had been arrested, tortured, and released twice on suspicion of assisting an outside force not compatible with the dictator's overall views. He had at great personal risk reported on foreign war material which he observed at the harbor being offloaded, the construction of the SAM sites, the PLO camps, and the introduction of Soviet troops in the country for many years. He had recently been severely compromised by Soviet agents who had reported his suspected activities to the internal security forces. He was currently in hiding with the Tuareg several hundred kilometers in the desert far south of the city where the agent would be inserted.

The Director concluded his long briefing by telling the agent that his initial contact in the eastern city of the country would be a Bangladeshi who had provided invaluable support to the Bedouin. He worked as a low-level staff member of the university. He was not trusted at the highest level; nevertheless, he was trusted enough to assist the agent because the Bedouin to be extracted had recruited him and used his connections successfully with no problems.

The agent would enter the country with an American passport, correct visa, and have a prearranged position at the university teaching English as a Second Language. He was to secure friendships with as many foreign and native instructors as possible. This action would possibly lead to new intelligence. He also was to visit often the large library looking for foreign adults there. It had long been suspected that various Soviet personnel frequented the library.

The Director did not offer any apologies for the complexity of this assignment. The only thing he added was that the physical demands would be great. He told the agent that, after the several initial tasks had been completed, he only then could make the complicated arrangements for the extraction with the understanding that Langley considered it both important and very demanding.

The agent spent the following day in a safe house in northern Virginia. He left the next day on a flight to London where he went to the American embassy to inquire whether there were any updates on his assignments After being told there were none, he boarded the afternoon flight to the country's capital. He was not surprised — because of his very thorough briefing — to hear Russian spoken on the airplane filled otherwise with citizens returning home. The two Russian men had, no doubt, been to their embassy in London with reports from the targeted country. In the event that Langley did not know of this conduit yet, he would go to the American embassy to let the station chief there know.

He went through emigration quickly and easily. The only question he was asked was whether or not he had any whiskey in his small carry-on. The official was pleased to hear him say no and welcomed him to his country. The taxi drive was inexpensive but lengthy. It took perhaps 70 minutes to reach the American embassy driving on the very crowded streets. He went into the embassy and reported to the station chief about the two men speaking Russian. He was told it had been suspected but not verified. The known exit flight used by the Russians left the eastern city to Athens. He thanked the agent for the new and useful information. He then invited the agent to spend the night with him in his small apartment. He said he would take the agent to the airport in the morning for his flight to the eastern city where he would be stationed.

The next morning he took the uneventful flight to the city where would acquaint himself with his new surroundings and slowly — always with purpose — meet people who could possibly assist him in any number of ways. He knew he would eventually meet the Bangladeshi at the university when he reported there for his prearranged position. He wondered how all the various pieces of a very large and dangerous puzzle would finally fit together: meeting the Bangladeshi; locating the PLO camp; infiltrating it; terminating the PLO commander; finding trusted Bedouins who could guide him deep into the Sahara to the location of the one to be extracted; and arranging for him to be securely extracted from the country. It seemed the director's comment that the extraction would be very demanding was a correct assessment.

After landing he, as the other passengers, had been almost rushed through emigration. He thought because it was

Ramadan and very hot that the officials preferred not talking and using vanishing energies to search people's luggage. He took a taxi to the hotel where he had been instructed to stay. The airport, small for such a large city with international workers, was about 25 kilometers from the hotel. The taxi driver was also not overly loquacious and did not offer to open the rear door for the agent. The hotel, a reminder of the country's past, was stately with large sitting and dining rooms, long veranda, and comfortable rooms. No wonder it had been called the Palace Hotel during the king's reign.

As he walked up to the hotel from the taxi, the first people whom he saw were Russians. They were sitting on the veranda drinking coffee and talking animately in Russian without any regard to who might hear them. He was surprised by what he saw and heard. He would attempt while at the hotel to obtain a rough estimate of the number of Russians in the city. He knew that not all of them would be staying in the hotel. He also wanted to see if there were any Soviets in uniforms in and around the city. Since he was fluent in Russian, he could eavesdrop on conversations both on the veranda and in the dining room. He hoped it would be possible, over time, to learn the names and location of the Soviet agents who had compromised the educated Bedouin. With those thoughts primarily on his mind, he took a long and refreshing walk along the corniche. He noticed that the majority of people walking were citizens and very few foreigners.

The next morning at breakfast in the very spacious dining room, he was approached several times by foreigners who had recognized that he had not been seen before in the dining room. He was careful to remember their names, nationalities, and jobs in the country. This was information which could be an asset to planning by Langley. Most were degreed workers in the oil industry; however, a few were university instructors and medical personnel. Many had brought their families with them. They were staying at the hotel until they could locate suitable housing.

Many were already complaining about restrictions on their lives. The impromptu meetings ceased after a few days when the other diners saw that he had not left and also because many of the people had begun to move to their housing. In some ways he was glad that the other diners saw that he had not left and also because many of the people had stoped approaching his table because he did not want any undue attention focused on him.

Since he had been requested by Langley to remain in his hotel for six days, he used those days to explore the city. He wanted to observe people, places, and general things so that he would feel more comfortable in his new surroundings. He knew that this varied information would assist him with the several required items which he had to do prior to the beginning of the extraction.

One late afternoon he took a taxi from the hotel to the stationery shop which the educated Bedouin whom he was tasked with to extract owned. It was located in a crowded and run-down section of the city. Opposite the shop was a small mosque for the neighborhood. Because he owned the rather large stationary shop which foreigners frequented to purchase otherwise unattainable items, the Bedouin (who spoke fluent English and German) was granted governmental permission to travel twice a year to Germany to purchase supplies to replenish his shop. He reported his information he had gathered from observations and conversations in person to Langley's station chief in the American embassy during the trips. This was invaluable since there was no middle person involved.

He had, unfortunately, been followed by Soviet agents on his last few trips. Those agents informed the internal security forces who had then arrested and tortured him. After having these actions done to him twice, he went into hiding several hundred kilometers into the Sahara. He was living with the nomadic Tuareg. His shop had been run in the meantime by two of his cousins.

The agent learned by a chance encounter on the hotel's veranda from an American couple the evening of the third day of his stay that a thoracic surgeon — the only one in the country — wanted to rent the rooms on the second floor of his house specifically to a westerner. The husband of the couple would be working in the medical school of the university, and he made arrangements for the agent to meet the surgeon the next day. The agent and surgeon agreed on the rent after pleasantries over cups of coffee. The agent told the surgeon he would move in two day's time.

His fifth day at the hotel was Friday. He knew the university would be free of students; so he took a taxi from the hotel the eight or so kilometers to the university. Even though he had seen Land Sat photos of it, he was surprised by both the size and modernity of it. He walked freely around the huge complex. He was able to able to verify the existence of the SAM site about two kilometers from the campus near the sea. The reality of it made startlingly clear the reports of the one he was to extract.

That afternoon he went by taxi to a used vehicle souk on the outskirts of the city which he had learned of from several of the guests at the hotel. He bought, after a few rounds of bargaining, a 128 Fiat four door sedan. He would use it to move his few belongings to the house of the surgeon as well as to drive around the city without having to take taxis. Since there was a large foreign community, he would be able to drive not only to their houses but also to go to their planned get-togethers. This would be an excellent method to hear discussions of life in the city. He eventually got to know many of the British, French, and Americans who lived and worked there. Most of them met every Friday for a picnic on various beaches near the city. They were often accompanied by native citizens who, as he quickly learned, were not at all sympathetic with the regime. He knew that some who went with the foreigners on their Friday outings would be informants. These he would definitely want to engage.

The following Monday he drove down to the university to obtain his needed credentials as an instructor of English as a Second Language as well as his library entry card. He had been told in his briefing that foreign agents frequented the library attempting to recruit foreigners. It was very important that he go to the huge library as often as he could. He was assigned a large office in the Faculty of Economics building along with the rosters of the students who would be attending his courses. He saw that, in addition to native students, many were from Egypt, the Sudan, and Iraq. These students would in time give him relevant information concerning the politics of the area in general. To make his appointment to the university complete, he opened a small checking account in the bank located near one of the entrances near the library. He met the dean of the faculty and also the chairman of his department both of whom welcomed him to the university.

He eventually met his Bangladeshi contact who, as expected, provided him with information concerning the PLO camp he was to infiltrate and the names of suspected native informants. He also suggested to the agent that he go to the English school where many parents from England and America enrolled their children. The Bangladeshi told him that the parents knew many natives whom they did not trust. This turned out to be quite true, and the agent gained from the parents much information which would have taken a long time for him to assemble. He met an archeologist with a PhD from Princeton at one of the Friday outings who — perhaps because of his trusted work for the Minister of the Interior — knew many people in the government. The agent also met a Coptic Christian from Egypt who worked in the medical school as a forensic pathologist. He was able to introduce the agent to many people both foreign and native. These contacts would prove to be invaluable.

He had been in the city for almost six months and had established many useful contacts. He was very carefully accomplishing the "many overlying factors" prior to beginning the extraction. What he had left to do were three important — and not to be left undone — items: infiltrate the PLO camp and terminate the commander; locate the Bedouins who could guide him to the Tuareg; and extract the subject. He knew he had to do each carefully and completely.

Using the intelligence from the Bangladeshi, he reconnoitered the PLO camp. The entrance was very heavily guarded. All who entered, including those delivering supplies such as food, were searched thoroughly without any exception. The only positive thing which he could ascertain from his several days of observation was that the entrance was across a busy street from several shops. He knew that, in spite of his dark tan, beard, local clothing, and fluency in Arabic, he would be unable to infiltrate the PLO camp through its main entrance. Through his many years of experience, he knew that all things — people or places — would always exhibit a weakness. He believed that the entrance was intended to show power and impregnability to all who drove or walked by. He further believed that the weakness of the PLO camp would be its perimeter far outside of the city. With that focus, he contacted the Bangladeshi who drove him south and east of the entrance for several kilometers in his old battered Peugeot pickup.

He found the weakness: the far end of the camp had only a few stands of barbed wire indicating a boundary from the few scattered houses there. It would be here that he would enter the camp. He waited until the evening of the next day to have the Bangladeshi drive him back to the same area. Before he got out of the pickup, the Bangladeshi handed him a vintage WWII .45 colt revolver and a scabbarded stiletto of dubious origin. He told the agent that, after he used them, to discard them in the camp. The agent fastened both around his waist using a cloth belt under his galabeya.

The agent wore a grayish and appropriately dirty galabeya with a few tears in it and also a red and white checked kufeya around his head. He wore old sandals which looked as though they had been worn all his adult life. With his deeply tanned face and hands and his full beard along with his fluency in Arabic, he would mix easily with the ones in the PLO camp. He knew that his appearance would not attract any undue attention. With that very assurance, he could put his full attention on locating the commander who would, no doubt, be accompanied by hangers - on hoping to curry favor.

He walked totally unimpeded and without any notice to the area where the old barracks were which housed the regular militants. He had been shown in his briefing close-up Land Sat photos pinpointing the most likely barrack where the commander would be housed. Unlike the other run-down barracks, his was made of concrete blocks with a courtyard in front of it with a rather large communal area where men could gather to eat, smoke, and talk. This was the place he needed to locate. Since everyone believed the entire area was completely secure, it was likely that the commander would be outside in the communal area in an ostentatious show indicating how they not only were safe from any interference but also able to do whatever they wanted. It was a simple message; however, when it was repeated often enough, the uneducated followers believed it without any questions.

As he came closer to the area where the commander's barrack was, he heard a cacophony of songs, jubilant shouts, and various arms being fired into the night sky. He saw men dancing in a ragged circle to the incessant beat of drums and tambourines. In the center of the make-shift circle was a large cooking area with several pots filled with water into which, without measuring, both rice and couscous were dumped. The pots were hung on tripods over the flames. Chunks of both mutton and camel were being grilled over other open flames.

The men attending the meals were also chanting and occasionally firing their weapons into the air. Huge platters with a mound of harissa in the middle of each lay on the ground. There were also several boxes of flat breads near the enormous platters.

The agent, because of his previous experience in the Middle East, knew that this was not a normal occurrence for an evening meal. There was little doubt but that the commander of the camp had made an unusual announcement earlier in the evening. Either something happened internationally which benefitted the PLO or an important person would be visiting the camp. He thought the latter was much more likely than the former. The commander used whatever news it was to provide his militants with an excuse to celebrate — and for a while to forget their regimented existence. They were confined to the camp with few opportunities to celebrate anything.

He soon heard from the jubilant men the reason for their celebration: Yasser Arafat would be arriving tomorrow afternoon. He was further told that the commander had learned of the pending arrival only a few hours earlier. He knew that when Arafat traveled, he almost never let his plans be made public. This meant that a runner/courier

had come to Benghazi with the announcement. He had heard prior to his arrival that Arafat was in Tunisia. There was no doubt that Langley knew of his movements but was unable to communicate this with the agent. That he now knew was one of those nuances field clandestine agents had to make use of as they occurred. He now had to spoil Arafat's arrival at the PLO camp by terminating the commander.

After he noticed that the circle of dancing and shouting men had grown to a chaotic and undulating group five deep, he joined it so that he would be on the outside. He would be able to observe the ones on the slightly elevated veranda in front of the commander's barrack. He saw that the commander was sitting with a small group after he had gone around twice. Most of the dancing and shouting men in the cumbersome circle were firing their weapons into the air. He knew that, with the amount of noise and erratic movements of the very excited militants, he would have his best opportunity to accomplish his first objective of his assignment: terminate the commander.

As the large and unorganized circle became noisier with the shouting of the militants firing their weapons, he knew this would be his only very good chance at the termination. As the circle came around the third time toward the veranda, he removed his old .45 Colt revolver from under his galabeya and fired it into the night sky. Since there were many weapons being fired, his action did not attract any attention. When he was perhaps 15 meters from the sitting commander, he fired his revolver at him. The heavy round struck the commander in the left side of his chest lifting him up and backward to the right out of his plastic chair. The agent quickly looked at the far side of the circle and saw that none of the shouting militants had noticed anything. He then dropped his revolver in the path of the dancing men next to him in the fourth circle. He also discarded his scabbarded stiletto a few meters away.

By the time he had danced his way to the far side of the large circle, he heard above the noise a crescendo of angry and very excited shouts coming from the ones who were on the veranda with the now dead commander. He heard loud orders for the gates of the camp to be opened. He knew that the two Toyota pickups with .50 caliber machine guns mounted in the beds would come roaring in when the heavy gates were pulled open. He knew that, in the midst of the total confusion, he could leave through the opened gates. He ran with perhaps 15 militants to help in pulling the gates open. As soon as the gates were pulled open and the two Toyota pickups accelerated in, he ran out and turned right down the street outside the gates.

Since it was almost 11:00 p.m. all the shops on the street

were closed with their metal shutters pulled down and locked. Most of the houses behind the customary tall walls had no lights on. He walked with purpose without showing haste in the event anyone driving by on the street noticed him. He stopped momentarily to take off both the galabeya and kufeya. After walking about two kilometers from the PLO camp, he threw both in an open trash cart. It took him a little over 45 minutes to walk to his house. He had not been stopped by any of the vehicles speeding toward the PLO camp. He had heard in the distance the sirens of ambulances rushing to the camp. Before he opened the outside gate to his house, he looked under the two concrete building blocks which he and the Bangladeshi had agreed upon to leave notes for each other. The note he found read simply that Arafat would be at the PLO camp tomorrow afternoon. This confirmed what he had heard inside the camp.

He met the Bangladeshi in the library the following afternoon. He was told that an arrangement had been made for him to meet two Bedouins in Ajdabiya in three days. He would find them at a cafe near the bus stop. They would guide him to the Tuareg after they met later in Sabha. They would explain to him the very difficult travel from Sabha to the Tuareg camp and also what he should wear.

He took the coastal bus three days later to Ajdabiya where he met the two Bedouins at the cafe. They were sitting outside smoking from a hookah. They were a father, Ahmed, and his son, Taher, pair who had many years of experience navigating the empty expanses of the Sahara. They explained to him the long and severe journey from Sabha to the Tuareg. There would be little water available along the way. What water they would have would be in goat skins. Each would have one, and the water would have to last until they reached the first oasis. They told him to make sure to bring several kilos of dates for his food. He was told to wear a white galabeya with a white kufeya around his head, face, and neck to protect him from the searing sun. They would each be riding a camel. They finally told him to meet them in six days on the northwest outskirts of Sabha by 8:00 p.m. They would leave after the sun had fully set and travel all night until they made their first camp some 12 hours later. The agent knew then that the two Bedouins were truly experienced since they would be navigating by stars.

He returned to Benghazi and explained to the Bangladeshi what he had been told. The agent told him he would take a bus from Benghazi to Surt; and then he would change to the desert bus going southward to Sabha. The Bangladeshi purchased for him the necessary bus tickets as well as two airline tickets for him and the educated Bedouin to fly from Sabha to Tripoli.

He left on the morning of the 5th day because he wanted not only to be on time for the 8:00 p.m. departure with the two Bedouins but also because he wanted to walk around Sabha listening for anti-government voices. He knew that he would have to bring the person to be extracted to Sabha in order to fly to Tripoli, and he wanted to ascertain the general mood of the desert city.

He got a room in a nondescript hotel with an attached cafe. He spent several hours listening to conversations at the cafe. He walked around Sabha the next day noticing the presence of government forces. He bought three kilos of dates for his journey and a woven bag to put them in. He walked to the northwest outskirts of the city as the two Bedouins had instructed him. He was not surprised to find that the area was a large encampment of traders buying and selling goats, sheep, camels, and the rare horse.

He met the two Bedouins who had three tall and lean camels which were definitely not cargo camels and were built for speed. They explained to him that it would be an approximate 30 hour ride to Bi'r de Sadi where they would have a ten hour rest before resuming an approximate 22 hour ride to

Uwaymat Wannin. There they would have an eight hour rest before going northward and slightly east for about 12 hours into the Hamadat Tinghert. There they would meet up with the Tinariwen — the "desert people" as they were known in Tamasheq, the language of the Tuareg. It would be a grueling 60 hour ride with only 23 hours of rest. He knew that they, because of their many trips into the Sahara, calculated what both their camels and they could tolerate.

They explained to him, prior to leaving at almost 8:00 p.m., that they would ride ten hours until 6:00 a.m. They would then have a four hour rest and begin again at 10:00am. They did not ask him if he were able to make the long journey; he realized they would not offer any assistance if he faltered in any manner. He knew his physical and mental abilities would be tested to their very limits.

The ten hours through the darkness of the Sahara went more quickly than he would have guessed. He soon adapted to the swaying rhythm of his seemingly indefatigable camel. He marveled at the constant speed and strength of it. They stopped at a tiny oasis at 6:00 a.m. where two groups of Bedouins were camped. They first watered their camels before they ate a simple meal of dates and bread. They refilled their goatskin water containers with the cool water from the oasis. They then rested four hours.

When he awoke from his deep four hour sleep, he heard a man shouting for mercy and begging for his life coming from the camp of the other Bedouins. He saw a man with a long rope around his neck which was tied to the saddle of a camel. The man's hands were tied behind his back. He had no clothes or sandals on. He asked Ahmed what was happening. Ahmed explained to him that the man had committed adultery and then killed the woman's husband. The harsh sentence was that he would be forced to walk in the searing heat of the day until he collapsed and then be dragged through the sand until he was dead. The woman would be left at the camp: if she survived fine; if not also fine. The agent asked no questions about the judgment concerning the two.

As they were packing, Ahmed told him that this next part of the journey would be the second most difficult one. They would ride all day until 8:00 p.m. He told the agent that, because of the distance involved between small oases, the timing simply could not be avoided. They would rest for five hours at their next stop from 8:00 p.m. to 1:00 a.m. They would then leave riding for ten hours from 1:00 a.m. until 10:00 a.m. They would rest at Bi'r as Sahi, a small village with a large oasis, for ten hours to allow their camels to recover from the 30 hour journey and also to regain their strength for the remaining 22 hours to the next village.

Those hours of riding in the relentless heat of the Sahara pushed him to the very limit of his considerable physical strength. When he approached exhaustion, all he had to do to continue was to observe both Ahmed and Taher as well as the camels and how they seemed never to tire.

After the ten hour rest at Bi'r as Sahi, the three riders and their camels were ready to make the 22 hour journey to Uwaymat Wannin. They had purchased more dates and bread for the next part of their tiring journey. They left at 8:00 p.m. and rode until 6:00 a.m. when they took a four hour rest. They now had to ride from 10:00 a.m. to 10:00 p.m. in the punishing heat. They could look forward to an eight hour rest in Uwaymat Wannin before they would leave at 6:00 p.m. riding north into the Hamadat Tinghert to meet the Tuareg around 2:00 p.m. The agent thought their ability to go through wholly empty stretches of Sahara — especially at night — was perhaps better than Land Sat photos to guide them. The precision of Ahmed and Taher never failed to amaze him; and neither did the seemingly never-ending strength of their camels.

As they finally approached the camp of the Tuareg, he saw that one of them rode toward them with a rifle aimed at him. Ahmed explained to him that this was an old custom and that he had nothing to fear. Ahmed made the introductions in guttural Tamasheq telling the Tuareg man that the stranger and they came in peace wishing only to secure the release of the Bedouin whom they had cared for so well and for so long. When Ahmed introduced the agent to the Tuareg man, the Tuareg expressed his admiration that the stranger had been able to make such a long journey. The agent knew he had gained their trust.

The Tuareg told them they could follow him to their camp where they could feed and rest their camels as well as being welcome to join them in a meal. He finally told them that the friend of the stranger would be found near the watering well in the small oasis. The agent thanked him for his many kindnesses. He also told the Tuareg that, if they had a camel to sell, he would pay a top price for it because he needed one for his friend to ride back to Sabha. The Tuareg promised that, Allah willing, all would be done.

The Bedouin to be extracted was, as they were told, near the watering well of the small oasis. The agent explained to him that he and the two Bedouins would assist him in leaving the country both without harm or notice. He told the Bedouin that they would leave in three days to Sabha. There they would part from Ahmed and Taher. He and the agent would fly the following day to Tripoli where the American embassy would provide him with a British passport containing all the appropriate visas and also a ticket to London.

The evening prior to Ahmed and Taher, the extracted Bedouin, and the agent leaving, the Tuareg killed two goats which they grilled using fully desiccated camel dung as fuel. They also exchanged gifts. The chief of the Tuareg gave the agent a large rug which they commonly used as a shade from the sun, to sleep on, and as a carry-all for their meager belongings. The agent gave the chief an 1884 American silver dollar which his mother had given him many years ago. The festivities went on until they left at 11:00 p.m.

They made the arduous journey back to the northwest outskirts of Sabha without incidence. He thanked Ahmed and Taher profusely for their gracious assistance. Though they were reluctant to accept the monetary gift of $500.00 each, he persuaded them to accept it after much sincere back and forth. The Bangladeshi, who had gotten the funds from the American embassy, had put the ten one hundred bills in a small silver-meshed purse which he had brought in a souk in Benghazi. After many masalamas — goodbyes —- and mutual blessings, they departed.

They flew from Sabha to Tripoli where he took the extracted Bedouin to the American embassy where he was provided with western clothes, a British passport, and a ticket to London. The agent briefed the station chief on his activities. He then flew back to Benghazi knowing he had accomplished the many overlying factors which the director at Langley had spoken of.

EMIGRATION OFFICE

Langley had sent him to a large American embassy located in central Europe where he was to meet a new clandestine agent. The new agent had just been assigned to this embassy and had not yet been given his first field assignment. Though he had gone successfully through extensive physical and mental training at the Farm, working alone in the field was something which could not be understood in spite of many months of arduous training. There not only were too many nuances inherent in field work but also there were the inevitable complications arising from unforeseen problems. And above all these elements was the exacting requirement that a clandestine field agent always — without any exception — worked under a very thick cloak of deniability; in other words if something went wrong with an assignment and the agent was implicated by the country in which he was working, Langley would deny not only any knowledge of the situation but also of the agent. This burden proved too onerous for some agents; only the very best ones accepted it without question.

When he met the new clandestine agent in the embassy, he was struck by how young the agent seemed. He wondered if that meant he had grown old-looking from his many years of clandestine work. It had definitely not made him look young he thought. His years of experience at least had kept him young physically and mentally. He knew that the new agent, if he were to be successful in the strenuous field work that he would eventually be assigned to, would have to be both flexible and purposeful in his approach to his assignments. The two descriptions were not incompatible: being flexible meant that he would have to have the mental ability to change a course of action; and being purposeful meant he would have to have the physical ability to remain on course.

Success would always mean having both abilities — there was no place for anything less. This demand was a fixed requirement.

The new agent had graduated from a small college in southern U.S. with high honors majoring in psychology with a minor in Russian. He had played football for four years. He fit well the mental and physical profiles which Langley looked for. All he needed now was some mentoring and a successful completion of his first assignment. The new agent asked many questions without being apprehensive about any of the answers. The agent summarized the three hour meeting with the new agent by emphasizing two points: to be truly successful, his work in the field as a clandestine agent had best be done without being noticed; and he should always strive to leave without anyone from his opposition knowing he had been there. Accomplishing these two objectives should become part of his career. The new agent agreed. He then asked Langley's agent how could one incorporate these two things into his field work. He was told without hesitation that they would become a part of him only with experience and error.

When he left the embassy, he knew he had ten days before he had to be at another American embassy to be briefed on his next assignment. Since he was near where he had been given his first assignment many years ago, he decided that he would visit the places as a tourist. He took a train to Pula where one of the best preserved Roman coliseums was. He remembered seeing it fleetingly years ago as he had been following all along the entire Adriatic coast an American who had sold information to the Soviet Union. Seeing it now without pressure of time constraints allowed him to marvel at the engineering skills of the Romans. He even had time now to enjoy a leisurely lunch at a small cafe'.

Rather than spending the night in Pula, he took a bus down the coast to Split where the magnificent ruins of Diocletian's palace were. He wandered among the ruins taking in for the first time what was surely an overwhelming presence many centuries ago. It even had its own harbor when the palace was first occupied. After spending several hours there, he boarded another bus which would take him down the coast to the Pearl of the Adriatic: Dubrovnik.

He looked forward to seeing the lovely place once again. Lord Byron had written that, if one had been there once, that person would return. He walked along the top of the wall surrounding the old town savoring the wonderful views. He also went into the old church where a Rembrandt was prominently displayed. He spent the night in Dubrovnik in a small bed and breakfast thankful that he had the time to do so.

As he journeyed on by bus to the small town of Ulcinj, his peaceful reverie was momentarily interrupted by the memory of the young American airman whom he had apprehended and extracted taking him back to Paris. He wondered what had eventually happened to him. He had lunch with a Muslim family who had invited him after he assisted their ten year old daughter in carrying several sacks of groceries to their little house on a hill overlooking both Ulcinj and the coast farther south.

Since the Albanian border was about 13 kilometers from Ulcinj and also because he had read in the International Herald Tribune that the American State Department had lifted the ban on American citizens going to Albania, he decided he would go. He rented a bicycle — Tito had famously allowed capitalism in Communist Yugoslavia to the extent that Yugoslavians would say that there were more communists in Italy than in their country — and rode to within two kilometers of the border where the narrow road abruptly ended and became a trail. All he saw on the road was one man shepherding his goats. The border was not only not guarded but had only a gate which a few people from each country freely used. He walked perhaps three kilometers into Albania and turned back because it had begun to rain.

When he was a few kilometers from Ulcinj on his rented bicycle, the rain had become a downpour. He saw a small house with a man standing in the door gesturing for him to come in. The house had only a dirt floor, but the comfort of the home with its warming fireplace and cups of Turkish coffee which the wife of the man prepared for him made him feel very welcomed. He was always thankful for the ones whom he met on his travels outside of his work. They reminded him through their kindnesses that there were good and honorable people in his small world.

After spending another night in Ulcinj, he took a bus to Ljublijana where he boarded a train and traveled to a large central European city. The morning after he arrived, he walked — as was his custom when in a new place — to the American embassy. By walking he was also to observe more closely both people and landmarks than if he had been in a taxi. He stopped once at a cafe' where he had coffee and read a local newspaper at a table outside. These seemingly innocuous actions provided him with valuable on-site information which gave him, often, a better sense of his new surroundings. Good clandestine agents made use of everything.

When he arrived at the American embassy, he was ushered to the office of Langley's station chief who still had the bearing of having been a Marine prior to his joining the Central Intelligence Agency. He had served six years in the Marine Corps after graduating from the Naval Academy. He was in his sixteenth year with the Agency. He had been posted on the average every two years to a different embassy. Though he often was brusque — some would say very curt — he cared deeply for the welfare of the clandestine agents to whom he gave assignments. He knew that what he had condensed from the analysts in Langley not only had to be accurate but also complete. Any variation from that could possibly harm a clandestine agent. The agents on assignment and the station chief ensconced in any embassy had to trust one another explicitly. Any deviation from a briefing would be made by the agent in the field if unforeseen conditions warranted a change. Even then trust still remained.

The station chief, in his usual direct way, began by telling the agent that he would be required to cross into the Russian sector of the deeply divided city. He would enter as a tourist wanting to see the magnificent Pergamon altar. He would be given a United Kingdom passport and present himself as an archeological historian from Merton College in Oxford. He was to stay in a pension for several days before beginning the extraction. The man and woman whom he would extract were currently in Warsaw. There were many indications that they had been compromised by a Polish double agent. Their extraction would be complicated the station chief explained; what they knew and from whom was vitally important to European security. The station chief emphasized the difficulty of meeting them at the Bahnhof when they arrived from Poland, and then the necessity of taking them to another pension without the ever-present security people noticing. He ended the briefing by telling the agent the most difficult part of this extraction assignment would be helping them — somehow without being obvious — in obtaining exit visas. He also said that each had different passports because each were citizens of different countries. This would present another problem for the agent.

After spending the night in the pension, he took a train to the crossing between the Allied and Russian sectors. He had been told at his briefing that, once he had crossed successfully, he was to find a pension in which to stay as a tourist. He would have that as his base until the two to be extracted had arrived. They had been informed in Warsaw that a person would meet them at the train station. He would then take them to the immigration office where he would assist them with obtaining their exit visas. The agent would also have to obtain his exit visa. One of the requirements in securing an exit visa was that anyone asking for such a visa had to leave that country through the same route which he had used to enter the country. An exit visa would not be given for a different destination. This would be relatively easy for the agent since he had entered a few days earlier as a tourist; however, the man and woman had been in Warsaw for several years and could not now show where they had previously entered the Deutsche Democratic Republic. The DDR kept very close tabs on who entered and exited. The agent would have to be both inventive and persuasive with the emigration officials.

He had been told at his briefing that, even though he wanted an entry visa as a tourist, he could expect to be thoroughly interrogated by the DDR officials since he was not a German wishing to visit relatives. He was taken to a small room where there were two Stasi officers. Standing behind them were two Russian officers. His small travel bag was first searched. They found the usual toiletries in addition to chicken grease-stained underwear: his pension has no hand towels. The only object they found which they deemed subversive was an old copy of the Reader's Digest which they kept. The DDR officers then began interrogating him. Every time they asked a question, he would answer in Russian. The Stasi quickly became annoyed while the Russian officers finally began laughing at the ones who were asking questions for not understanding Russian.

After he was released from the interrogation room, he was given his tourist entry visa. Even though it was mid-December and cold with light snow falling, he decided he would walk to the pension whose address Langley had given him. As he walked the almost deserted streets in the Russian sector, he was surprised by how many buildings had not been repaired from the damage cause by the Allied bombing during WWII. Many of the buildings, including the once magnificent Reichstag building, had fences erected around their ruins. It seemed that not only the government of the DDR but also its Russian ally did not want to invest funds in the repair of the buildings. The only movements on the streets were old trams and a few belching Trabant cars.

He finally stopped at a small cafe' where he had coffee and a surprisingly good wiener schnitzel with sauerkraut. The little cafe' also had a selection of picture post cards depicting what once was the city prior to the devastation and also some of Soviet memorials. He bought one which had a photo of the museum where the Pergamon altar was. He bought that one and mailed it to his parents using DDR stamps which he had purchased in the emigration office. He wanted them to believe he was here as a tourist. The subterfuge was perhaps not truly good, but it was necessary in order to reassure his parents. It also served to protect them from knowing anything about his work.

He then walked to his pension which was owned by a very old German couple. Over an evening of small glasses of cognac, he learned that both of their children had been able to leave in the months following the death of Hitler and before the Russians had established a firm position in their city. They both lived in Milwaukee in the large German community. The old parents told him they were too old to leave and that all they had was the pension which brought in enough Reichmarks for them to live well enough. He offered to pay them in Western currency, but they refused telling him it would be far too much trouble — and explanations — for them to convert it to Reichmarks. He told them he understood their quandary.

Since he had two days before the couple would arrive by

train from Warsaw, he spent the next day both walking and riding trams around the dilapidated and austere city. He went into several shops and found the shelves basically bare. There were always queues outside of both bakeries and butcher shops. There was simply no good comparison with the western sector of the city. The only truly outstanding thing the eastern sector had to offer was the lovely Pergamon altar. When he saw it in the late afternoon, he realized that the photographs he had seen of it in his only art history class he took at the university were underwhelming. The glory and grandeur were without adequate description by any means of representation. He bought two postal cards in the kiosk near the entrance of the museum. One was a close-up of the altar and the other one was a longer view. He mailed both of them to his parents.

He took a crowded tram to the Bahnhof where he walked around inside so that he could both familiarize himself with the exits and also locate the gate where the train with the two people to be extracted would arrive. He, through his years of experience, additionally closely observed the people around him. He noticed that there were many armed eastern sector security people in the station. Most of the people waiting for the train seemed anxious. He knew they were hoping that they would not be stopped and questioned by one of the security people. He could only imagine their daily frustrations as they attempted to eke out some semblance of what should be normal. All of these burdens could lead someday, he thought, to a far-reaching revolution.

When he went out on the platform to meet the train, he found that it had become cold with an eastern wind blowing the heavy snow in gusting swirls. The train appeared out of the snow with its headlights gleaming and the large red hammer and sickle illuminated on its front. As the train came to a hissing halt, he began walking down the platform stopping about half way so that he could observe both toward the front and rear of the multi-carriage passenger train. He knew the couple had been told to wait for a while before getting off. This served two good purposes: the platform crowds would have thinned out; and it would give him a much better opportunity to see them at a distance. Neither they nor he could afford missing one another. Far too much depended on their meeting not to get together. He had been shown their photos at his briefing; so he would be able recognize them. They had been told that a man would approach them and ask how their parents were. They would answer that they just came back from a holiday in Majorca. He had also been told in his briefing that they were seasoned agents and not novices.

Both had been embedded in communist Poland for several years. They had lived in Gdansk in an apartment overlooking the seaport. There they could see all the nationalities of arriving cargo ships. They also were able to catalog any military vehicles on the decks of the ships. They then were told to move to Warsaw to an apartment on the outskirts of the city near a military depot which also housed very large barracks of soldiers. They were able eventually to report approximately how many soldiers were in the garrison in addition to how many Soviet troops were there with the Polish ones. Their most important information which they faithfully reported over several years was the detailed movements of Soviet troops and war materiel from the U.S.S.R. and how often these occurred. These reports were invaluable both to the U.S. and NATO. They had, unfortunately, been severely compromised by a Polish double agent. They had to be extracted before their arrests. Langley believed they would now be closely watched and followed. He had to make certain that their meeting on the platform had the look and feel of relatives meetings. It was a certainty that at least two surveillance personnel would have been assigned to follow them. He would have to be able to lose them in the large and crowded visa area in the emigration hall.

He finally saw the man and woman exiting their carriage. Before he approached them, he waited until he could identify any security people who had traveled with them. After a few more passengers had gotten off the train, he saw two men looking intently in the direction where their charges had walked. Both — mainly because of the austere security in the country — made no attempt to conceal what they were doing and what their purpose was. When passengers on the platform saw them, they gave the two men a wide berth. The two who were to be extracted did not go toward him. Their years of experience told them to wait until Langley's agent approached them. The two security men walked perhaps 20 meters behind the man and woman. They did not want the ones they had to watch out of their sight. He walked up to the man and woman and asked loudly enough that the security detail heard him ask how their parents were. Without missing a beat, they answered — also loudly — that their parents had just arrived home from their holiday in Majorca. He could tell from the look in their eyes that they were very relieved he had identified them.

The two agents were in their late thirties but looked much older because of their many years of dangerous work. Being embedded was fraught with daily difficulties. They also appeared haggard, no doubt, because of their having been compromised by the double agent. After having been compromised less than a year ago, they had been forced to leave their small apartment and move from one pension to another in an attempt not to be arrested. They were finally informed by an agent of Langley's who worked with them in Warsaw that their usefulness had deteriorated and that their continued presence was detrimental to the overall work which needed to be done. They were then assisted with obtaining both train tickets and exit visas from Poland. They were to travel to the Soviet sector of the divided city. There, they were told, an agent from Langley would assist them in getting to the West. They were also told that their extractions would be difficult; but because of their value to the U.S.A., the extractions would be handled by one of Langley's very best agents.

The man and woman had met at a large university in northern Europe. Both had studied political science. They were married after they graduated. They got positions in an import firm. There they were recruited by Langley to do undercover work in eastern Poland. They very quickly proved themselves to be excellent assets. They had very good memories and were never excessive in their daily lives. They each had administrative positions in the import firm. There they were able to see what the country was importing and from where.

As he walked with them from the train's platform and then across the street to the emigration hall, he knew the two who had been assigned to follow them would be very careful in not letting them out of their sight. His only hope was that, when they were separated in the cavernous room where the visa departments were, the two security men would be momentarily confused. It would be then that he would be able to lose them in the crowded and chaotic room. He doubted very much that the two had ever been in this particular situation before. Often the security people from eastern Poland had never been out of the country much less been confronted with a scene such as the emigration office serving so many eastern and western travelers.

As he had been told in his briefing, another difficulty was that each of the two being extracted had to go to separate exit visa departments. The man was an eastern European from Estonia, and the woman was a western European from Greece. They had to obtain exit visas from two different offices. He had to assist them in getting their exit visas without being noticed by the ones following them. Since he also needed an exit visa, he would go first with the man to the office handling exit visas for eastern travelers. This visa approval would be much more difficult than for the woman. He would then get his exit visa when he took the woman to the office handling exit visas for western travelers.

It was easy to pretend to bump into the man and woman in the loud and crowded hall. He quickly told the man to follow him and told the woman to wait near the circular information desk. When the man was approved for his exit visa, he told him to wait outside in the small plaza until he and the woman came out to join him. He told them both that, if they all became separated, they were to take a tram to the border sector; walk through the checkpoint and wait for him on the other side. He told them that, although it would be time-consuming, everything should go well. He told them finally to be aware as much as possible of the two security people following them.

As he was taking the Estonian man to the exit visa office, he noticed that the two security personnel had ceased following the man and were standing near the woman. He hoped that she would not move from the information desk — and if spoken to, would answer only in Greek. He could not watch her as he and the man slowly went through the crowds of people in the hall. When they got to the exit visa office for eastern Europeans, they found a long queue of anxious people wanting for their turn. He noticed that several Stasi were very openly taking photos of all who were standing in line. Since he could not be photographed with the one to be extracted, he told him to meet at the information desk after he received his exit visa.

After he made his way to the information desk, he saw that the woman was not there. To make a difficult situation worse, the two security men also were not there. He realized that they had probably made a clumsy, but forceful, attempt at abducting her. He had to locate her which meant he had to move around the huge and now even more crowded hall. He hoped the Estonian would still go to the information desk after he got his exit visa. All being separated was his main concern now. He had somehow to find not only the woman but also the two security men who now, no doubt, were with her.

Unknown to the agent was what had happened to the

Estonian when he finally was interviewed for his exit visa. He was questioned repeatedly about wanting a visa to the West and why he did not want an exit visa to his home country of Estonia. He was also asked why his wife was a Greek and how he met her. The ones doing the interrogation wanted to know why both had lived so long in Poland. What were they doing there was asked often. Since they had lived in Poland so long, why were they now wanting to leave for the West was another repeated question. The officials also wanted to know where he and his wife would be living in the West. They also wanted to know from him if he and his wife would be doing the same kind of work in the West. Their final question to him was why did they leave such good positions in the import firm. The Stasi, not being satisfied with most of his answers, told him he would be placed in a holding room while they sent telegrams to the authorities in Warsaw and also the import form. Until they received what they deemed satisfactory answers, he would not be given an exit visa.

The agent began his arduous walk through the crowd of people in the large arrival hall. It was difficult not only to move easily but also to see because of the huge number of packed-in weary travelers waiting and hoping for their turn to obtain exit visas. The noise was overwhelmingly cacophonous with irritated exclamations in many languages. There was no order to anything which resulted in the enormous mass of people moving in no particular direction. After making his laborious way back to the information desk which was besieged by people wanting to know where to go and what to do, he decided that he would search the perimeter of the hall. He figured he would have a better chance of finding the Greek woman there rather than in the crowd of sweating and tired people. As he moved slowly along the perimeter, he saw only old people either leaning against the wall or trying to find a place to sit on the floor with their battered suitcases. He did not see her, and he had traversed more than half the hall's perimeter. He was now convinced that she had been taken somewhere in the hall. Both she and the two security men would be prohibited from leaving either the exit or entry doors of the hall; so this was a solid indication to him that they were still somewhere inside.

He continued his search along the perimeter all the while paying close attention to the Stasi who were watching intently the people in the hall. They always rebuffed any inquiries from anyone who approached them seeking information. They were not tourists guides; they were there to prevent any attempts at leaving the hall. None of them were young, and all appeared seasoned veterans at keeping order. He noticed quickly their pattern: as some would force their way across the floor, others would take their place along the perimeter. He timed how long the replacements took — about four to six minutes because of the increasingly packed hall. This knowledge would help him when he found the Greek woman. Those precious minutes would afford him the time to move her into the melee of people thus helping to remove her from the scrutiny of the two following her.

When he had gone almost all the way around the perimeter without finding her, he knew it would be close to impossible to locate her in the crowed arrival hall away from the perimeter. There numbered, he estimated, perhaps 600 people in the hall. The ones on the outside would be prevented from entering because it would take the rest of the day to process the ones already in. Those outside would have to endure not only the snowy and windy cold but also the total lack of restrooms. They were at the mercy of the slow DDR bureaucracy who had little regard for any suffering humans.

Since his progress was impeded, he stopped for a moment near the open door leading to the men's restroom. The line to enter was full of struggling, sweating, and exasperated men cursing in as many languages as the proverbial tower of Babel. Some, having given up hope of getting inside the restroom, were openly urinating on the stinking floor. The Stasi, as implacable as ever, looked on with disgust without saying anything.

All of a sudden, there was screaming coming from the women's restroom. Women were pushing their way out trampling on the slower and older women. All had horrified looks in their faces. People in the chaotic hall nearest the women's restroom tried to push their way into the already overcrowded throngs in the hall. Those farthest away either did not hear the commotion or did not care. As the shoving and screaming women, some with infants, continued pressing their way out into the hall without regard to those who were in their way, an enormous and unmovable group of terrified women quickly accumulated. The Stasi could not — and did not — ignore this. Several bulled their way to the outer edge of the pile nearest the hall and began to pick up and throw women onto the mass of people in the hall without any thought to the safety of anyone.

He knew without any remaining doubt that he had located the Greek woman. He fought his way into the women's restroom attempting not to harm anyone. By the time he had reached the area of the stalls, the restroom had been emptied of women. What he saw did not surprise him. One of the security men was holding the woman in a chokehold while the other was about to inject her with a long-needled syringe into her exposed neck. He immediately kicked the one with the syringe up under his jaw hard enough to break his neck. That one was dead before he fell to the floor. The other man let go of the women and stepped toward the agent who hit him with a vicious karate chop to his left jugular causing the security man to drop at once.

He took the woman by her right arm and began forcing their way out of the corridor into the hall. He kept close to the wall knowing that at the entrance he would go to the right away from where he had observed the Stasi clearing the mass of women. He knew that, if he could get to the perimeter, they had a very good chance of disappearing into the throng of people. He also knew that the chaos caused by the screaming women would assist them. Even the Stasi would see that it was a man helping a woman and would think it was a husband helping his wife. He told her that it was absolutely imperative that they not become separated. They reached the entrance to the women's restroom and turned right along the perimeter. After going several meters, he told her they would now make their way through the crowd toward the exit visa office she would be using. He also told her that her husband had possibly been delayed in receiving his exit visa. He told her that he could not be certain of that. He finally told her that, since both she and he needed western exit visas, they would go together to the exit visa office. Once they had received their exit visas, they would go outside and wait in the plaza near the tram stop for her husband to join them.

Still unknown to the agent was the status of her husband. He hoped the Estonian would remember to meet them outside the building — and if they were not there, to take the tram to the sector's border and wait for them there.

The man waited for more than two hours for the Stasi holding him in a room near the exit visa area to receive the two telegrams. He had been further questioned concerning how he met his wife and were satisfied when he told them they had met at the university where they were studying. He told the stern interrogators that they had accepted their jobs at the import firm because they had gotten married and needed work. He told them they had lived all the years in Poland because they felt that the Polish government took care of its citizens. They had finally left because his wife's parents in Greece were old and needed help. And, yes, they hoped to get similar positions in an import term in Athens. He showed the Stasi his Polish exit visa and his paid-for train tickets to Berlin. Fortunately for him all of this was collaborated by the telegrams from both his former employer and the Polish authorities. Reluctantly and with barely suppressed annoyance, he was given his exit visa. He knew he was late and probably could not immediately reunite with his wife and the agent; however, if he could not find them outside, he would take a tram to the sector's border.

The agent and the Greek woman walked together through the packed hall to the western visa office. He told her to go first, and then to wait for him in the plaza near the tram station. He also told her that, if they became separated, to take a tram to the sector's border where he would meet her — and with any luck her husband would also be there. In the event all became separated because of the crowd near the tram station, she was to go through customs and then take a tram to the pension whose address he had given to both of them.

When the Greek woman obtained her exit visa, she went to the plaza as instructed. After waiting for almost 45 minutes with no sign of either her husband or the agent, she went through customs and then to the tram station on the western side where she continued her wait for the two missing men. She knew that her husband would likely have had difficulty getting his visa; so she decided to wait for at least an hour. She hoped the agent would appear with her husband.

After the agent had secured his exit visa, he had to exchange basically worthless DDR currency for Deutsche marks because he held a western passport. He then went as quickly as he could out to the plaza knowing that neither the Estonian nor the Greek would probably not be there. They were not. So now his hope was that they would not be separated; and, if so, that they each could make it to the pension.

The Estonian waited at the tram station outside the arrival hall for perhaps 30 minutes. After he could not find his wife or see the agent, he took a tram to the sector's border where he went through customs easily. He walked to the tram station and watched again for his wife and the agent. Not finding them, he took a tram as he had been instructed to the pension.

The Greek woman finally gave up hope on finding her husband or the agent at the tram station. It was becoming dark with snow now falling heavily. She did not like the stares of men who found themselves free of the communist east. She had heard too many stories of women being kidnapped once they were out of the arrival hall for her to wait any longer. She got on the tram which would take her to the pension where she hoped her husband and agent were.

The agent knew there were many possibilities for the husband and wife to become separated outside the arrival hall. Additionally he knew that the western sector was full of foreign agents from many countries all looking for tired, and sometimes confused, people who had traveled from the east to the west. These people were vulnerable to the polished greetings of the agents who would promise them almost anything in order to gain their confidence. Many of the travelers had both little funds and nowhere to stay. A well-trained agent could ensnare those quickly by preying on their obvious needs. Women were especially targeted.

The Estonian now knew that all three had become separated as he rode the tram to the pension. He had waited until he was certain that neither his wife nor the agent could be seen anywhere. He knew that, because of their years serving as embedded agents, his wife would be able to handle this particular situation.

The Greek woman was approached several times at the tram station by men whom she surmised were foreign agents. She brushed them off by saying she was going to meet her husband. One agent insisted that he accompany her on the tram telling her that he would protect her from any harm. She told him that she really did not want his offer. She also told him that if he persisted, she would notify the tram driver. He then left her alone.

The agent had to wait for 20 minutes for the next tram. He had not been able to see either of the two whom he had to extract. He noticed after he boarded the tram that there were several men — whom he recognized by their mannerisms — who were without any doubt foreign agents. He found it unprofessional what they were attempting even though he knew they were doing what they had been told to do.

When all three were safely reunited in the pension, he told them he would take them to the American consulate where they would be given train tickets to a large city in the west. They would be accompanied by someone from the consulate. Once they had been partially debriefed at the American embassy in the city where they were going, they would be furnished with airplane tickets to the U.S. Once again, he told them, they would be accompanied by someone to ensure their safe arrival in America. They had no questions, but were greatly relieved to hear what the agent told them. They thanked him profusely for what he had done for them.

He only smiled; said rest well tonight; and then went to his room.

THE PRISONER

Even though Prisoner Number 1442 lay wracked in indescribable pain stuffed in a six by three by two feet concrete box with an inch thick iron lid fastened with shackles covering the entire top with only three air holes located somewhere in a god-forsaken desert in a small village where shouts of angry men and grunts of camels were all to be heard, he refused to die. His dreams did not cease, and his hope never failed him. Perhaps more importantly, his faithful memories sustained him even when delirium would invade his consciousness. The splattering of his blood during horrific hours of inhumane torture reminded him of a red rose in his mother's garden so many long years ago when he was young and wholly innocent of geo-political intrigues.

> *He wanted to pick one perfect red rose for his mother to place in the old vase which she kept so carefully on the mantle above the fireplace.*
>
> *He cut the red rose with a long stem, removing the thorns so that his mother would not be pricked, early one morning. The dew on the rose made the fragrance even more enhanced.*
>
> *He took it into the kitchen lean-to where his mother was making biscuits for breakfast. When he gave it to her, she hugged him tightly with her floured hands and thanked him over and over.*

She poured water from the drinking bucket into her old vase and carefully placed the red rose on the mantle above the fireplace in the log cabin.

The red rose lasted, with its pervading fragrance, for many days.

He had been given an almost impossible assignment: he was to infiltrate a large terrorist cell; assassinate the cell's leader and his chief lieutenant; seize computer files; and leave undetected back to the one square kilometer pickup zone which was approximately 20 kilometers away from the cell's encampment. The satellite photos he had carefully memorized clearly showed the size of the compound, the heavily guarded perimeter, the mud brick building where the targets and computers were, and the two small villages between the drop-off and his destination. The houses of the villages were simple abodes. Each village had a water well around which dogs lay.

The hand-dug well supplied his family with abundant water year round. Everyone took their turn at drawing a bucket of water for the house. The water was clear and cold. Milk and cream from their Jersey cow were lowered into the well until they just touched the cold water. Without electricity this was their refrigeration.

When his mother did the weekly washing, many buckets had to be drawn in order to fill the outdoor wash pot under which a fire was built to heat the cold water of the well. All would help her empty the hot water into a wash tub where his mother would laboriously clean the patched jeans, shirts, and other items with a rub board.

The cleaned clothes would then be rinsed in a smaller wash tub and hung out to dry on the clothes line. Being dried outside even on cloudy days, imbued their laundry with a fresh fragrance.

The helicopter used to drop him off had advanced noise-cancelling equipment both for the rotors and engine; it had flown low from its base some 200 kilometers away without being seen or heard. The landing was soft and uneventful – and on time at 12:30 a.m. The crew said nothing as he exited the ship. He did not watch as it flew silently away. By the time it had gained its low operating altitude, he had already sprinted almost a kilometer into the moonless desert toward the first village. He had to get past both villages during the very early morning when all would be sleeping, and the night's temperature in the desert caused the inhabitants to sleep deeply.

The fireplace and cook stove were the only sources of heat in the full-of-wind-entering cracks in their house during cold winters. Ice always formed in the drinking bucket overnight where a long-handled dipper for communal use was placed. Only after the embers in the fireplace and cook stove were used to start the day's fires would the ice melt.

He was armed with a well-silenced Uzi pistol with a large magazine and a 12 inch sheathed knife. Both were fastened tightly around his waist and tied to his thighs so that there would be no movement of either as he ran relentlessly toward his target.

He wore black form-fitting pants and shirt both of which had no pockets. He shoes were ankle length, lightweight and also black. He knew he had to move quickly and quietly taking advantage of the darkness and the early hours of the day. His night vision goggles helped him immensely. He had to be at the compound by 2:30 a.m. He had been given one hour to infiltrate and two hours to return to the landing zone.

The two small villages would have to be skirted cautiously, even though there would be no armed patrols near them, because of the constant presence of dogs. He hoped they would be asleep lying around the wells of the two villages near the drinking troughs.

He easily ran past the first village without being noticed. By the time he had gone past the second village, he noticed that the morning's cooking fires had not yet begun; so he knew the inhabitants were still asleep.

The wood-burning cook stove in the small lean-to attached to the log cabin served the family of five both as a stove where simple but filling meals were cooked and as a heating source.

The lean-to was used as a kitchen and dining area. In the small room was a round pedestaled wooden table around which were three old cane-bottomed chairs where his mother, brother, and sister sat. He and his father sat on a home-made bench fashioned from a one inch thick by one foot wide by six feet long slab gotten from the local sawmill.

The table was also used as a place where his mother would prepare meals and wash dishes in a wash pan after meals. It additionally was where he did his homework in the evenings.

He knew from the sat photos that, approximately 50 meters from the compound, there would be two armed guards in each quadrant around the entire area. There would be in addition two armed guards at the door of the target. There would also be as usual several dogs by the well which was about 30 meters form the entrance of the house.

As he approached the eastern quadrant, he slowed down to a careful, quiet, and measured walk. He became acutely aware of what was on the parched ground. He could make no noise which might arouse the two armed guards who were about 20 meters apart. He found them, as he thought, sound asleep. He waited only a few minutes observing them before moving silently toward the empty space around the building.

He knew that the empty space would be the most difficult part of his approach. The area around the target's house was devoid of everything with the exception of four scrub bushes somehow living in the dried soil. He quickly noticed that the three dogs were asleep near the well. With the exception of the rustling of the tethered camels, there were no sounds anywhere.

He began his slow and cautious move across the barren space being especially certain he did not step on anything which might make a sound. The dogs were to his left about 20 meters away. They remained asleep as he took in the sight of the two armed guards. They were about 10 meters each from either side of the door. They were slumped over asleep with their backs against the wall of the house. Their AK-47s were propped at arm's length against the house.

Both guards were young and very thin. He did not want to kill them. They had been conscripted into a thankless job. They would remain as guards until they were captured, killed, or dismissed by the leader. He knew they had little hope for a good future. He wanted them to remain asleep as he approached the door.

The house was a low-slung square building perhaps three meters high made of large rocks and small stones over which was a dirt plaster which had faded to a bland brown which caused the small and windowless house to blend well with its surrounding. He knew from memory the landmarks of the façade of the house. What the sat photos did not reveal, however, was the stench of urine and feces near the building.

The door was about two meters high and perhaps one and a half meters wide. It was made of wood with metal bracings running diagonally across the door. There was no latch or handle on it. There were four wide leather hinges which supported the door. It could be opened from the outside only by pushing on it. There were openings at the top and bottom the width of the door of about five centimeters.

He was now very thankful for his night vision goggles. He silently was thankful for the invention. He could see the two guards and, if they had been awake, could not see him. Both were snoring and looked helpless. Their snoring would cover any creaks of the door when he opened it.

> *When he and his brother were nine and ten years old, they decided to walk approximately seven kilometers through the dense forest; cross a small stream; and approach their grandparents' house through a field of wild sunflowers. They wanted to see if they could walk without disturbing any wildlife and eventually surprising their grandparents.*
>
> *The route they chose included two steep hills on each side of the stream. They knew that squirrels, rabbits, birds, and perhaps a deer or two would be along their path. They would have to walk cautiously if they were to make the trip without the wildlife noticing them.*
>
> *Going down one slippery hill, crossing the stream, and going up the opposite slippery hill was difficult, but they managed well and did not disturb any wildlife.*
>
> *As he and his brother approached the clearing outside of the woods and just before the field of wild sunflowers, they noticed a doe with her fawn feeding perhaps 30 meters from them. The animals were in their direct path. They waited patiently without moving until the doe and fawn went back into the sheltering woods.*
>
> *They then crossed the clearing and went into the field of wild sunflowers. The fragrance of the leaves*

and the buzzing of various bees filled their senses as they moved through the field toward the gate opening into their grandparents' yard. They opened the gate without making any noise, and were able to cross the yard to the porch where their grandfather was sitting without being noticed.

He moved silently and swiftly to the door. He hoped the opening of it would make no sound. He pushed on the door, and it barely made a sound. He opened it enough so that he could both enter and leave easily.

The interior of the windowless room was surprisingly cool; however, the odors of sweat, urine, and cigarette smoke were truly fetid. The laptop computer was on a small table near the target's cot. The room was utterly devoid of anything one might expect in a well-used living quarter.

The target was lying on his back with his right arm bent above his bearded face and unkempt hair. His left arm was down by his side. His lieutenant was lying on his side with his arms bent near his bearded face. Both were snoring and sound asleep.

He unholstered his Uzi pistol and shot the target in the center of his forehead. He died immediately making no sound. He shot the lieutenant in his temple. The only sound he made was a slight and harsh intake of breath.

He re-holstered his Uzi pistol. He quickly placed the laptop in his black tote bag leaving through the opening of the door silently. The two young guards and the dogs were still asleep.

From the moment he opened the door until he left took less than 15 seconds.

When he was 15, his mother asked him to go squirrel hunting so that the family would have meat for supper. He took his single shot 22 caliber Remington rifle with one shell chambered and one more in the pocket of his jeans. He wore his well-used engineer boots. He wanted to go to a large group of oak trees with lots of acorns which he knew from experience the squirrels would be eating.

In order to get there, he had to traverse a craggy outcrop of flat and loose rocks which not only would make his footing difficult but also harbor lizards and other creatures which would startle less knowledgeable hunters. He had gone up almost to the top when he heard before seeing it a coiled timber rattlesnake ready to strike his left foot about a meter away.

He stopped and did not move until he knew where to place his feet back a few steps. He then chambered his shell and shot the rattlesnake in the head. While it was writhing, he quickly went around the area until he had reached the top.

He went quietly toward the stand of acorn-laden oak trees stopping only to chamber his remaining shell. Soon he saw a squirrel silhouetted on a limb perhaps 20 meters high. He shot it cleanly through its head, and was able to return home with the evening's meat for his family.

He left the compound retracing the path he had entered it. He went through the same quadrant and found the two guards still sound asleep. He was able to leave the area totally undetected. He knew, however, that he had to get past the two villages before he could begin to relax mentally.

He sprinted toward the far outskirts of the nearest village being very careful not to go close to it even though doing so would save him precious time. So far he was ahead of the well-planned schedule. His being at the LZ slightly before his pick-up would greatly assist the chopper's crew. Everyone depended on his elusive abilities to carry out the very detailed operation.

He went past the first village's guards and dogs without incident. As he continued to sprint toward the far outskirts of the second village, he knew there could be someone awake. Though the momentary temptation to go far outside his path was great, he knew that doing that would add too much time to his arrival and cause him to be late for the pick-up. It had been scheduled down to the minute, and any deviation from that would put all at risk. He continued sprinting along the same way he had come in. With his night vision goggles, he was able to see clearly any obstacles in his way.

Part of the well-rehearsed plan was for him to observe, find, and use any places where he could conceal separately his black tote bag with the important laptop and his Uzi pistol, knife, and goggles in the event he was discovered. It was vitally important that he could carry out these actions even as potential captors were approaching.

He saw as he came near the second village that the two guards had moved. This could mean anything from their going to the well for a drink to expanding their patrol radius. He knew he had to be very vigilant to sounds and movements the guards might make. He also began taking close notice of depressions where he could place and cover his very valuable possessions.

Suddenly he heard dogs barking, and then saw one of the guards 30 or so meters to his left. He was much more concerned about the dogs than the guard who could not see him in the darkness. He could outrun the guard; but the dogs would rapidly overtake him and attack him. He decided to continue sprinting hoping the dogs would have difficulty sniffing his presence in the breezeless early morning.

The other guard now appeared perhaps 40 meters directly in front of him. Both guards were moving slowly in a vector toward him without realizing that he was in their vicinity. The dogs were jumping about between the moving guards barking loudly in their frustration at not being able to smell anything out of the ordinary.

Even though he was more than three-quarters of the way past the village, he knew he could never avoid the dogs. The guards were stumbling in the complete darkness and would miss him if not for the dogs. While he hoped for the best, he knew that getting away from the dogs would be almost impossible. When the dogs found him, the guards would quickly arrive.

He would now have to hide quickly and well what he had with him. He remembered a depression a few meters back where he could place the tote bag with the laptop. He turned; found the depression; put the tote bag in it; and placed flat rocks over them. To his right 10 meters away was a small but long pile of sand where he dug a hole large enough to put the Uzi pistol, knife, and goggle in. He covered them as best as he could. He then sprinted faster than before to the right of the second guard who by now had closed the distance to about 20 meters. The first guard had fallen and was trying to get up all the while urging the dogs to run ahead of him toward the second guard.

He knew he would be unable to outrun the pack of dogs even with his track speed. When they attacked him, two of the dogs clamped down on his legs while the other three immediately jumped on his back pulling him down. They were relentless in their attack, and did not cease even when the two guards began beating him with their stubby AK-47s.

Barely conscious, he felt the tethering ropes being tied to his arms above his wrists. The two guards began pulling him on his back toward the village. As soon as they got him to the village, men came out and began beating him on his face, chest, stomach, and legs with the hardened prodding sticks used to direct their camels and donkeys.

Before he mercifully lost consciousness, he heard excited and angry shouts that the leader and his helper had been killed. This caused even more vicious beatings. What he could not have known because he became unconscious is that he was dragged on his back while being beaten and stabbed all the way to the compound. There he was dumped into the concrete coffin to rot in the suffocating heat lying in his blood.

When he was a senior in high school, he was the basketball's team leader in rebounds, assists, steals, and second in points. He also had a 97.3 percent from the free throw line. His team, because of its outstanding record of 19-0, had been invited to an at-large invitational tournament where all classifications would be playing.

With six seconds remaining in the championship game and with his team one point behind, he got a defensive rebound. As he came down, he was elbowed in the face which split his lower lip and also caused him to bite his tongue. As he bent over still clutching his rebound, a player from the other team kneed him in his lower posterior causing him to fall to the gym's floor. A third player pretending he was stumbling kicked him in his solar plexus.

He was given a one and one. His coach wanted to remove him from the game because of his injuries, but he adamantly said no knowing that none of the reserves could make the free throws. With blood flowing off his chin and the pain from the kicks coursing through his body, he made the first free throw which tied the game. He then sank the second one which won for his tiny high school (19 in his graduating class) the invitational tournament. The trophy and his MVP trophy still remain in the school's trophy case.

His team won because he refused to quit. This characteristic was with him his entire life.

When he did not return to the designated pick-up area, a coordinated series of search and rescue plans were put together. He had to be rescued or his body retrieved along with the important laptop. New sat photos – well-enlarged – were made; a cruise missile was programmed to the coordinates of the compound; jet fighters were on high alert stand-by; a unit of the Delta Force would be inserted in a heavily armed Black Hawk copter with a medic on board.

On the 53rd hour of his entombment dying from loss of blood and lack of water, a cruise missile slammed into the compound followed by strafing runs by the jets. Soon the Black Hawk landed with the Delta Force unit laying down a suppressing and merciless blanket of heavy fire.

He was jarred into consciousness from his delirium by the unmistakable sounds of the attack. Pieces of shrapnel and rocks rained on and against the concrete coffin which, ironically, now protected him. His tortured body was willed by his mind and spirit to remain calm. He knew he would eventually be rescued.

As he fought to remain conscious, he thought he heard the shackles of the top being unlocked. Slowly with grating sounds, the top was pushed open at the end where his swollen head was. Finally the top was pushed open about a third of the way in a diagonal. For the first time since he was thrown into the coffin, he smelled air that was not fetid with the odors of his lacerated body.

Then the face of what he thought must have been an angel appeared in the opening staring at him without saying a word. It was, in fact, the face of a young boy perhaps 12 years old. The boy showed mercy and strength far beyond his age. He then disappeared.

He wanted more than anything to summon his remaining strength and will to overcome the pain of his beaten body and pull himself out of the coffin. He managed with great difficulty to get one arm up to the edge and move his body so that he could begin pulling himself up one painful inch at a time. When he had turned enough to get his other arm onto the edge, he attempted to move his torso. He was unable to pull his torso up at first because of the indescribable pain.

With great difficulty he finally was able to sit up in the opening. Using his last bit of strength and will he pulled his body up and out of the coffin. As his body passed over the edge, he fell out screaming in pain from his broken ribs. He then blacked out. When he regained consciousness, he began to pull himself on the ground one inch by agonizing inch.

He had pulled his tortured body about three meters when he became aware of someone bending over him saying that he is safe now because we are here. He remembered attempting to tell the figure that the laptop was in his black tote bag in a depression near the first village. He remembered little else of his rescue until he was in a hospital many hours later.

When he was growing up, he attended Sunday school in a one-room country church. On Sunday mornings he and a few other boys would take two old hand-made benches out of the building and place them under the tall pine trees in the un-mown grass near the church. There ticks from the roaming cows would crawl up their legs. It was often difficult to pay attention to the old lady who taught them the Sunday school lessons.

One Sunday stood out, however, in his memory because of what the old lady, full of experience and knowledge, told the boys. Even though her dentures sounded like castanets clapping, her lesson this time made a profound impression on him.

She told the boys in a firm but kind manner that they would face problems in their lives from which there would seem to be no way out. She explained that they would likely encounter people who would be angels of whom they would not be aware who would help them.

She ended her lesson by saying slowly that God promised in Isaiah that He would cut in sunder the bars of iron which might occur in their lives. He never forgot that.

It was determined in the hospital that he had suffered seven broken ribs, lacerated liver and spleen, deep muscle contusions in his thighs and arms, and many other injuries. His black tote bag with the laptop and his Uzi pistol, knife, and goggles were retrieved.

His hope and his memories and his strength never failed him. He was successful in his assignment because he refused to give up.